## KILLER-ARMY ON THE MOVE . . .

Jane had to stop the scream that welled in her throat. Martinez was slumped over the wheel. His hands still grasped it, grasped it with such fierceness that the skin was taut enough for the bones of his knuckles to almost pierce through. His eyes were still wide open and on his face was frozen an expression of hideous anguish. His lips had been so chewed that they were lacerated and bloody. But the face was a death mask.

It was then that Jane noticed the lower half of his body. Nausea swept in waves through her body and she had to turn away to give vent to her feelings. The bottom of Martinez' legs appeared to have been eaten away. The flesh was mangled and bloody and in some places the bones stood through glistening white. Only some fierce determination had kept the old man at the wheel of his beloved *Falcão* until he died where he stood . . .

Also by Peter Tremayne in Sphere Books

THE VENGEANCE OF SHE

# The Ants

**PETER TREMAYNE**

SPHERE BOOKS LIMITED
30/32 Gray's Inn Road, London WC1X 8JL

For Tom and Elsie Charles in gratitude.

How far that little candle throws his beams!
So shines a good dead in a naughty world.

    William Shakespeare, *Merchant of Venice* Act V.

# CHAPTER ONE

The forest was strangely and disturbingly silent.

Tamāia the hunter paused beneath a tall hardwood *camioa* tree in a small clearing and peered about him suspiciously. To the forest-bred, silence means danger. All the usual background sounds, which the *caraibas* or European would take for granted or not even notice, were missing. Tamāia could not hear the scampering chatter of the small red-fur howler monkeys which usually screeched warnings of man's presence and often made a hunter's life hard to bear; he could not hear the distant bark of some hungry jaguar in search of prey; nor could he hear the varied bird songs or the tell-tale rustle of the undergrowth that would mark the passage of a deer, a *capybaras* or wild pig or even some smaller animal such as an armadillo or an anteater. Even the very wind itself seemed to have paused in its whispering passage through the topmost boughs of the great primeval rain forest.

The silence was complete.

Tamāia raised one hand to finger his magic charm, a coloured stone that hung on a thong of gut around his neck. His other hand gripped his *tacape*, a heavy wood cudgel, more tightly.

He was no coward but the forest silence was unnerving. He had only once before heard a silence faintly approaching this completeness. When he was a young boy he had been caught in the path of a forest fire. The animals had fled but the silence which they had left had been broken by the crash and crackling of the approaching flames. No, on reflection, this silence was a new experience for Tamāia.

He drew himself up to his full five feet. Tamāia was of the Trumái tribe and tall by their standards. His body gleamed a coppery bronze and he wore his jet black hair long. He was clad only in an *apí*, a string of vegetable fibre which wrapped around his penis and then continued upward in loose spirals to encircle his neck before returning again in

I

loose spirals to its point of departure. His only other adornment was his charm, bought from a *pajé*, an old witchdoctor, for a small bag of *patacat*, a variety of round bean much prized among the Trumái. Usually he went abroad in the forest with a short spear, which he cast from a sling, but today he had come from his village bearing only his cudgel for he was not hunting.

Reports had reached the Trumái that the Igaranhá, a fearful, malevolent spirit, was loose in the jungle and eating up all before it. The fearful spirit had been roused, it was said, because a great and oddly coloured bird, in whose gigantic body strange men flew, had roared down out of the sky, crashing into the forest and destroying the trees and causing great fires. The great bird lay dead, its body broken into many parts. But the bird had awoken the Igaranhá who was now angry with the world. The tribal elders had ordered Tamãia, who was the bravest warrier and greatest hunter of the tribe, to go forth and ascertain whether the reports were true and whether the evil spirit of the Igaranhá could be propitiated by suitable sacrifice.

As Tamãia had gone further and further into the great rain forests the sounds of nature had gradually died. Only once had he seen a living creature in the past half hour and that was only Urubu, the bald, black Brazilian vulture.

Now the silence was so complete that Tamãia shuddered in apprehension. Perhaps he was standing in the very presence of the Igaranhá himself? He peered about fearfully, gripping both charm and cudgel in tight fists.

Tamãia ran the tip of his tongue around his dry lips and coughed gently to ease the constriction of his throat.

'O Igaranhá!' he cried, his voice fading into the gloom of the forest. Tamãia waited a while, all the time peering into the darkness of the trees, at the maze of blue-green undergrowth with its riot of multi-coloured flowers. Still there was an uncanny silence.

'O Igaranhá, if your children, the Trumái, have offended you, tell me how we may make amends. I, your servant, Tamãia, will convey your wishes to the council of elders.'

But there was no answer from the Igaranhá.

Mentally, Tamãia prayed for protection to the spirit of

2

Jakuí, his own personal guardian and the chief of all spirits who live at the bottom of the rivers and lagoons.

What should he do? Go on? Move further into the forest in his search for the Igaranhá? Or should he go back to his village and tell them that the Igaranhá had not deigned to talk with him? Hesitantly, he moved further into the clearing.

Suddenly he was aware of a sound; a sound that he could not place, that he had never heard before. It was a high pitched sound, like the voices of young girls singing. No, it was pitched on a higher key than that. It was a tinkling sound like the tiny bells that the *caraibas'* religious men and women used in their ceremonies. Tamāia frowned. The missionaries had warned the Trumái of terrible consequences if they did not turn from their gods and worship the *caraibas'* god Cristo. The Trumái had listened politely to the missionaries, agreed with them, and after they had left had gone on worshipping the gods of the forest as they had done for centuries. Were the *caraibas* returning with their god Cristo to punish them?

Tamāia had no sooner registered the thought than he was aware of the fact that the high pitched sound was unpleasant in his ears. It was penetrating beyond his ears, eating into his temples, into his head, into his very brain, like a million tiny splinters of wood. Tiny, sharp prickings. He gave a small moan and reached a hand up to massage his brow.

The sound was all round him now, growing louder and louder, hurting his head more and more.

Tamāia was frightened. He was convinced that the *caraibas'* god Cristo had come to punish him even as the religious men of the *caraibas* had foretold. He called loudly on Jukuí to come to his protection and, in spite of the pain in his head, he straightened his body and raised his *tacape* in a defensive attitude.

Around the edges of the clearing the undergrowth swayed and rustled.

Tamāia's eyes widened in horror. He stepped backward involuntarily and then, after a second's pause, he turned to flee. But the noise was all around him. Angry! Malevolent! Without pity! He was cut off. In a split second Tamāia the

3

hunter saw the inevitability of his death. He raised his head and gave one long anguished cry.

'Jukuí!'

A few moments later there lay in the clearing a glistening white human skeleton. There was nothing to identify who it had been save for a coloured stone hung on a piece of gut around its neck and, by one skeletal hand, a cudgel.

The clearing was deserted.

The forest was strangely and disturbingly silent.

## CHAPTER TWO

Everyone knew Martinez' boat, the old *Falcão* or Falcon. At least all those who lived along the banks of the River Xingu below Von Martius Falls as far south as Morená where the river divided into a multitude of tributaries and lagoons across the flat region of tall treed, primeval rain forests which formed the northern part of the Matto Grosso, the largest of the twenty-two states which made up the Federal Republic of Brazil.

Martinez and his boat were quite an institution. Even the oldest settler could not remember a time when he had not heard the sound of three shrill shrieks from a steam whistle heralding the appearance of the *Falcão*, wallowing around some bend in the river, loaded with goods for trade or with passengers who would use the boat as the only means of transport through the inaccessible and little explored region. From the indian tribes of the Xingu to the Brazilian settlers, Martinez provided the link with the outside world.

The territory along the Xingu was sparsely populated by white settlers or, indeed, with indigenous indians. Many of the tribes had never even seen a white man. If the rest of Brazil regarded the Matto Grosso as remote, then this was the remotest region of the Matto Grosso; a region of thick inaccessible forests much of which had never been explored at all. A forward thinking Brazilian Government had, in 1961, designated the entire area of eleven thousand five hundred square miles as a national park in which to form a natural reservation as evidence of the state of Brazil at the time of its discovery by Europeans, to protect the fauna and flora of the area and the indigenous tribes of the region, offering them a chance to defend themselves from premature and harmful contact with white Brazilian society.

Apart from the indians who constituted some fourteen known tribes the handful of white residents consisted of government officials, a few traders like Martinez, teachers and missionaries. There were also a few hunters, with special licence and strict instructions on keeping an ecological balance. But dotted sparsely around the territory were several big estates which had been carved out of the jungle years before the Xingu area became a 'reserved' territory and for which the Brazilian Government had not been able to decide on a compensation scheme for their white owners. And so these estates had been left, usually producing rubber, cocoa or manganese. It had been easy to ignore them rather than come to grips with the problem.

Once a month, at least, Martinez and the *Falcão* put in at Morená where the *prefeitos* office was, which governed the district. Then he would head south towards the more inhospitable regions to trade, to deliver goods to the people crazy enough to live downriver. He worked his boat aided by two Xingu indians whom – unable to pronounce their real names – he called Primus and Secundus.

On this trip Martinez had only two passengers to transport down river . . . and one of those was a girl. Martinez spat reflectively in the shelter of his wheelhouse. Crazy people, both of them. *Louco!* Only crazy people would go voluntarily into the forests of the Xingu.

'The forest is beautiful, isn't it?'

Captain Orlando Villas paused in the act of lighting his cheroot and gazed quizzically at the eager face of the young woman who stood by his side at the rail of the old river boat. He followed the appreciative gaze of her grey-blue eyes as they took in the tall trees of the great, impenetrable rain forests on either bank. Villas let his eyes return to the smiling face of the girl, lit his cheroot and inhaled with a gentle sigh.

'*Sim*, senhorinha,' he agreed, 'It is very beautiful but also very ugly.'

The word '*repulsivo*' in Portuguese conveyed many things – the brutal savagery of nature as well as its magnificence.

The girl nodded slightly.

'I know what you mean, Captain, but it is beautiful nevertheless.'

The girl spoke Portuguese with an accent that Villas found hard to place. It was certainly not a north American accent and yet the girl spoke English as her mother tongue, of that he was sure.

Physically, she could certainly be an *Americanos*. She was tall with a graceful figure (Villas breathed a soft '*beleza*') although the waist, he reflected, was perhaps low and the hips were rather broad like many of Nordic origin. Her ash-blonde hair and grey-blue eyes contrasted vividly with the deep tan of an unblemished skin. The eyes were very attractive though they were set wide apart and had a knack of staring unblinkingly at you as if with an expression of total innocence. The mouth was a generous one, dimpled in the corners so that any expression other than a smile did not sit well on her features. Her clothes, too, were suggestive of an *Americanos*. Tight white shorts, displaying well shaped legs, a white safari jacket worn loosely over a similarly coloured blouse. White socks came below her knees and on her feet were sensible boots. Villas found the policeman in him deciding that the girl had been in the jungle before for the boots had obviously seen previous service. Yes, he pondered, she could pass for an *Americanos* but for the accent.

'The senhorinha is not American?' he enquired politely.

'English,' smiled the girl and added, unnecessarily, 'from England.'

'Ah,' a smile of understanding crept round the young captain's mustachioed lip. 'You must be the Senhorinha Sewell.'

Jane Sewell only just recognised her name from Villas' attempted pronunciation.

'That's right. But how . . .?'

'Permit me,' Captain Villas gave a half bow, 'I am Captain

6

Orlando Villas of the *prefeitos* at Morená. This,' he swept a hand towards the forest, 'is now my territory. I am the police commander of the area.'

Jane frowned.

'But there was another officer, a lieutenant . . .'

Villas pulled a face.

'Lieutenant Alfonso de Beja. Yes, he was in charge of the area. Did you know him?'

'Slightly, but what happened to him?'

'He was on a routine patrol in the country of the Trumái about a month ago. He has disappeared.'

'Disappeared? But how?'

Villas shrugged.

'Who can tell, senhorinha? A jaguar? A snake? There are many ways to disappear in the jungles of the Matto Grosso.'

The girl bit her lip.

'I only met him twice but he seemed so young for such a responsibility.'

'Now I have taken over the territory and it is my job to try to find him, senhorinha.'

The girl gazed at the captain for a moment.

'But how did you know who I was?'

'I have already met your father, Doctor Sewell, *não e*, is it not so? He told me that he and his daughter, Jane, had been working among the Trumái tribe for some months and that his daughter had gone to the capital, Cuiaba, to send back the results of their findings to England and that she would be returning to join him again soon. You and your father are . . . what is the word? . . . ah, yes, anthropologists, *não e*?'

Jane nodded.

'When did you see my father?'

'Two weeks ago as I was coming down river to Morená, senhorinha.'

'Is he well?'

'But certainly, senhorinha, and looking forward to your arrival. But you will excuse me for my impertinence. You do not look like a woman of science.'

Jane laughed at the captain. He was a good looking man

of thirty, handsome in a dark saturnine way and very *gallant*. She found herself thinking in the Portuguese idiom.

'*Obrigado, capitão*,' she smiled. 'But I am, indeed, a woman of science. I have been helping my father in his researches on the South American indians ever since I left university four years ago.'

Villas mentally congratulated himself in placing her age at about twenty-six years.

'And what is this work you do now, among the Trumái?'

'My father and I are trying to collect all the myths and legends of the tribes of the Xingu indians who live in this area. My father has been working among them for four months now. I spent the first two months with him and then I went up to Cuiaba with all our material for typing, collating and sending to the Institute of Social Anthropology in London . . .'

'Your pardon, senhorinha, the Institute of . . .?'

'The institute which finances our researches, captain.'

'And so now you are rejoining your father?'

'Yes.'

'And did you like well your stay in Cuiaba?'

The capital of the Matto Grosso state was hardly a place to enjoy, thought Jane. She had little to do in her spare time except avoid the advances of the young Brazilian men, attracted by her blonde hair and grey-blue eyes which made her a rarity in the city.

'I liked it well enough,' she replied indifferently.

'I confess, senhorinha, I find your occupation an odd one for a woman.'

He saw her start to open her mouth and raised a silencing hand.

'I confess, I am a prisoner of my culture. Here, in the Matto Grosso, time passes us by and we develop slowly. Perhaps God is to be thanked for that. Perhaps it is a virtue.'

Jane smiled.

'I am sure the indians would agree with you on that subject, captain.'

Villas' mouth quirked in answering amusement. He threw away the remnant of his cheroot.

'Ah senhorinha, I detect that you wish to protect the

8

indians from the white man's civilisation, *não e*, is it not so? Well, I agree with you. Every time we bring civilisation to the indians we merely introduce them to a plan for their destruction. Instead of help, education and good counsel all we succeed in passing onto them is our dislikes, prejudices, diseases and drink. We take their lands and corrupt the morality of their women, we destroy their culture and call it internationalising them. In the end our civilising of the indian means that they merely take the white man's vices and add them to their own vices.'

Jane stared in surprise at the police captain.

Villas grinned boyishly.

'Do not be surprised, senhorinha. A man has time to contemplate on many things here in the Matto Grosso when he has to police thousands of square miles of country which has so few inhabitants. There is little to do but study the people who surround him.'

'It seems an odd way for a policeman to pass his time . . . philosophising about the merits of civilisation.'

Villas grimaced.

'Ah, but I am not left to my own contemplation all the time. First there is the tragic business of Lieutenant de Beja. And now, today, I have to go up to the Bakirí country.'

Jane knew that the Bakirí tribe occupied a territory several miles upriver from the village where her father had his camp.

'What outbreak of lawlessness has happened among the Bakirí,' she asked with a touch of irony for the Bakirí were well known as a shy and inoffensive community.

'The *prefeitos* received a peculiar report that the Bakirí are moving out of the territory, moving further south. Also, and there may be no connection, it was on the borders of the Bakirí territory that Lieutenant de Beja was last seen.'

Jane frowned.

'But the Bakirí have lived in that territory for centuries. Why would they just move?'

Villas shrugged in a characteristic Latin manner.

'That, Senhorinha Sewell, is my mission to find out. We had a report some six weeks ago, before de Beja disappeared, that a United States bomber was forced down in the area.

9

But no one has located its exact position and the crew have been given up for dead. Perhaps the Bakirí found it and, not understanding it, have been frightened into leaving the area, regarding it as something magical. But who knows?'

Suddenly the stillness was pierced by three shrill blasts on the *Falcão*'s steam whistle. The old boat started to draw into the bank towards what seemed to be a pile of old logs heaped casually by the embankment. Closer inspection showed them to be a crudely constructed jetty.

'Ponto Paulo, senhorinha,' sang out Martinez from his wheelhouse.

Jane peered at the landing point and was disappointed not to see her father waiting for her. Strangely, for the arrival of the *Falcão* was always a big event on the river, there were no indians on the jetty to welcome them either. The little landing place was deserted. Of course, the village was a mile inshore. The indians of this part do not make a habit of building their villages on the banks of a big river, for in the rainy season floods can cause untold damage. Perhaps word had not reached her father of the coming of the *Falcão* although it was odd for she knew that long before the chugging of the *Falcão*'s engine became audible the news of its progress along the river would be swiftly passed from tribe to tribe. Doctor Sewell, and the tribe in which he had his camp, would surely have known of the approach of the boat at least an hour before it bumped against the wooden jetty which an enterprising bureaucrat in the capital had designated 'Ponto Paulo' on his map.

Martinez brought the old river boat wallowing up to the side of the makeshift wooden jetty while the two indian hands leapt ashore to make the vessel fast with ropes. Martinez left the engine idling while he climbed down to join Captain Villas and the girl.

'Odd,' he said, surveying the deserted clearing around the jetty. 'It's the first time I've known indians not to turn out to greet the old *Falcão*.'

'Well, it does not matter Commandante Martinez,' replied the girl. Everyone addressed Martinez as Commandante because, aside from being the owner and captain of his boat, it was also known that he had seen service in the Brazilian

Navy, although, if the truth were known, his rank hardly rose above that of a chief stoker. Martinez liked respect and even men like Captain Villas paid him the compliment of the title. 'No,' continued the girl, 'they may be at some religious ceremony. It is not too far for me to walk to the village by myself. I'll just leave my luggage here and go on.'

'Senhorinha,' interposed Villas, 'we cannot permit this. A young lady alone in the jungle . . . why, *Deus nos*, God forbid!'

'Nonsense!' rejoined Jane firmly. 'I am fully capable of taking care of myself, Captain. It is only a mile to the village and the path is broad and quite clear. There is no danger of me wandering from it. The predatory animals know it is a man made roadway and stay clear of it, so the dangers are minimal. Not only that, I am bound to meet my father coming to meet me for he will have heard by now of the *Falcão*'s coming. There is no need to worry over me.'

Villas bit his lip. In the face of the girl's determination, he seemed undecided.

'It is true what the English senhorinha says, captain,' said Martinez. 'Probably by the time we unload her baggage, her father will be here. But anyway, as she says, it is but a short distance to the village and there is little danger along the path. I know it well. Also,' he gave an apologetic grimace towards Jane, 'also, captain, you want to reach Ponto Bakirí before nightfall, *não e*?'

Villas nodded unwillingly.

'Very well. Regretfully, senhorinha, my mission makes me want to press on. It is against my nature to leave you unprotected . . .'

Jane Sewell gave a broad smile and laid a hand on Villas' sleeve.

'You are a little old fashioned, captain. But I am grateful for it. Please do not worry about me.'

Villas bowed.

'On the contrary, senhorinha. When the mission is accomplished I shall take the liberty of calling upon your father and yourself.'

'We will be pleased to see you, captain.'

Jane stood by her baggage, which the two indian hands

had placed by some trees away from the jetty, and watched as the *Falcão* disappeared round the bend in the river. Her last sight of the boat was of Captain Orlando Villas giving her a wave from the stern rail. She smiled softly to herself. Captain Villas was certainly good looking, if one went in for the dark, Latin type. But he was incredibly 'correct' and old fashioned in his manners and attitudes. As he said, time in many ways passed the people of the Matto Grosso by. She shrugged and dismissed Captain Villas from her mind.

She bent down and picked up what she termed as her 'emergency kit'. A few months in the Brazilian rain forests had taught her never to move far without carrying a haversack containing emergency rations, medical kit, compass, map and other necessities. It had become an automatic action that, whenever she was going to move far from camp, she swung the haversack on her shoulders.

Having done so, she peered along the path which led to the indian village. There was no movement along it. It was strange. Surely they knew she was there and had told her father? The only thing she could think of was that they might be engaged in some religious ritual which required the attendance of the entire tribe.

She looked at her baggage and then down the pathway, chewing her lips in indecision.

Then, squaring her shoulders, she took three paces down the path before halting. She returned to her baggage, bent down and opened one of the cases. From it she took a Sharpe's Express hunting rifle, a 0.303 calibre, and a box of ammunition. It was always well to be prepared, she told herself as she loaded ten rounds into the gun, placing the rest of the ammunition in her haversack.

Feeling more confident, she set off towards the village.

## CHAPTER THREE

Once away from the clearing by the riverside, the tall trees began to hem in on the pathway and create an atmosphere of gloom, shrouding the path in a strange half light. Now and again a shaft of sunlight would flicker through the waving branches of the trees, or shine steadily down with a strange beam-like quality where nature had allowed a small clearing to develop amidst the great wooden pillars of the forest.

The pathway, which ran to the side of a tiny stream that eventually emptied itself into the river, was a well worn trackway and Jane, who had travelled along it several times with her father, had no difficulty in following the route. The feet of the indians stamping the pathway clear over the centuries.

Jane walked at her ease, her rifle tucked in the crook of her arm, expecting at any moment to see her father, or some of the tribe with which they were staying, hurrying along to meet her.

But a strange quiet pervaded the forest.

Once or twice Jane stopped to listen. In the distance she could hear the excited jabbering of monkeys and, high above her, birds wheeled and shrilled. But it seemed to her that the forest sounds were strangely muted. Perhaps it was merely her imagination. After all, she had been away in a city for several weeks.

She began to walk on, perhaps a little more quickly than before, unable to shake off a feeling of unease which had started to grow at the back of her mind.

The familiar must and bitter-sweet smell of rotting vegetation began to assail her nostrils as she went further into the forest.

Her eyes began to pick out familiar landmarks along the path. There were the group of *pindaíba* trees, a sort of palm from which the indians from the village made their ropes. Here was a small clearing overgrown with *sapé*, a long reed like grass which was used to thatch the haystack like huts of the village. Indeed, the village itself could not be that far away for there was the old *Uaoacaêp* hardwood tree which the villagers brought offerings to because they believed that a spirit named Tavariri lived within it and must be regularly appeased with gifts.

And still there was no sign of a welcoming party. It was also unusual not to meet at least one indian on the path to the river. She halted again and listened. Only the faint screech of the bald vulture, wheeling in great spirals in search of food, echoed through the silent trees. If the villagers were engaged in some religious festival surely she would hear them by now? Jane felt her apprehension growing.

Hurrying forward she soon burst out of the gloom of the forest into a large rocky clearing where the stream fed several pools formed by hollows in the great rocks. It was in this clearing that the Trumái had chosen to make their village, a large settlement of nearly thirty sun baked mud brick huts, topped with their distinctive pointed thatched roofs.

Jane came to an abrupt halt and peered at the huts which spread in a disorderly fashion across the clearing, almost meandering towards the traditional *ocaríp* or centre square of the village which consisted of a cleared area of hardened earth. Overshadowing all the huts was a tall building which fronted this square in which dwelt the spirit of Jakuí and in which the elders of the village gathered in council with the chief.

The village seemed deserted.

Jane could see no fires, no people, no movement at all.

'Hello!' she cried, letting her voice linger over the last syllable of the word.

A silence greeted her.

She repeated the cry in the Xingu tongue.

Again there was a silence.

She moved forward slowly and came to the *ocaríp*. The large central fire of the village had been allowed to die out. Jane bent down and placed a hand over the whitened ashes. There was no heat. She touched them. They were cold. It was strange, unthinkable that the villagers would let the central fire go out.

She whirled round as a rustling movement came from the house of the Jakuí, as the council house was known.

Nervously, she raised her rifle to waist level and let her fingers curl around the trigger guard, her fore finger ready to slip against the trigger at a moment's notice.

'Is there anyone there?' she cried, still speaking in Xingu.

14

Again there was no answer.

Softly she moved forward to the entrance of the great hut and paused at the door to give her eyes time to adjust to the gloomy interior. Then she stepped through the doorway.

'Who's there?' she snapped, her voice cracking in her tension.

There was a sudden screeching and a red fur howler monkey went leaping towards a hole in the thatch and was gone into the forest.

Jane leant back against the wall of the hut, her heart beating a resounding tattoo against her ribs. She found that her face and palms of her hands were covered in perspiration.

She breathed deeply to regulate her breathing then drew back her shoulders and peered around the musty interior of the great hut.

It was deserted. The sparse furnishings were spread about in some disorder and the beautifully carved flutes and masks, which the Trumái used for religious ceremonies and always stored in the central hut, were scattered and smashed all over the floor. It seemed that the howler monkey had done its work of vandalism well.

An awful dread began to overcome Jane as she examined the deserted building.

The village was deserted. Why? Where was her father? And the words of Captain Villas echoed in a small corner of her mind. He was going a few miles downriver to investigate reports that the Bakirí had moved from their territory. Had the villagers here fled from their territory as well? And if so, what was the reason? And, above all, where *was* her father?

She pushed out of the hut and stood blinking in the reddy rays of the sun which was now balancing on the tops of the trees towards the western side of the clearing. It would soon be dark, for darkness comes in the tropical rain forests with amazing swiftness.

'Hello? Hello?' she cried again, making the word strangled as she pushed it from a throat dry with tension.

The silence was oppressive.

She moved foward to the hut in which her father lived.

In contrast to the central hut, it was fairly orderly. Only a sleeping bag was flung carelessly aside as if her father had been roused from his sleep, scrambling from his bag and leaving it discarded. A frown creased her brow. There were her father's clothes lying across a camp stool, neatly placed as was his custom before going to bed. She also became aware that an old lamp was still flickering on the wooden table, the flame smouldering across the last drops of oil before, even as she looked, it faded into extinction. And there was her father's rifle lying at the door of the hut as if thrown carelessly aside.

It was not like her father to be so careless with firearms.

A kaleidoscope of thoughts and images flashed through her mind. But Jane Sewell was basically a level-headed girl and not given to flights of fancy or panic. She suppressed the feelings of eerie dread that gnawed within her.

Her first job was to ascertain that the village was, indeed, deserted. She left her father's hut and went carefully around each one of the huts examining them closely and finding in some signs of precipitous flight. The villagers had certainly not prepared for their evacuation and, in several instances, had dropped things and fled, or so Jane conjectured. In some cases food, now decomposing in the fetid jungle atmosphere, had been left in the middle of a meal. One thing was certain . . . no villager had remained.

The sun had now sunk behind the tree tops and the clearing was shrouded in that brief moment of twilight that heralded the complete blackness of the tropical night.

Jane found a small can of paraffin in a corner of her father's hut and filled the hurricane lamp before relighting it. Then she set to examining his papers, books and diaries for some clue to the mysterious disappearance. The last entry in her father's diary had been made six days before and merely referred to an elaborate feast that had been held in honour of the chief spirit Jukuí. She turned from her task and made a brief inspection of her father's baggage without success. It was then that another puzzling thought struck her. She could not find any of her father's clothes missing. What, then, was he wearing?

She suppressed a shudder as the mystery took on a sinister aspect.

Had the village been attacked by another tribe? She knew

16

there were still several uncontacted tribes in the great forests around the Xingu and some of these still had a warlike disposition. Had some warrior society raided the village and carried off the Trumái and her father as well? It was not possible. She would have found signs of a struggle, arrows embedded in the huts or some other signs. Some indians would surely have been killed in such an attack. Yet there was no sign at all.

No, it seemed that the villagers, including her father, had gone one night; had gone hurriedly but had gone of their own free will.

She bit her lip in perplexity.

There was no more to be done until the morning. No more to be done, perhaps, until the return of Martinez and the *Falcão* with Captain Villas. Perhaps he would be able to furnish a clue to the mystery. He would probably be able to pick up a tracker and find which way her father and the villagers had gone. Perhaps her father, was for some reason, taking the tribe up river to Morená. But for what reason? There *must* be a reason. Indians did not leave their territory in which they had lived for countless generations for no reason at all. And why had her father gone in nothing more than his pyjamas, leaving all his papers, his rifle and personal effects in the hut? Her eyes fell on his shaving tackle, carefully placed on a shelf below a precariously perched mirror.

A feeling of some inexplicable terror suddenly seized her. She felt like running from the hut and back down the path to the river away from this oppressively silent and deserted village.

'I will not be hysterical,' she whispered fiercely to herself. 'I will not!'

She went to the door of the hut and peered out. The blackness of the night was so complete that she could hardly see the start of the forest, only a slight change in the degree of blackness, in the depths of the shadows, gave her any indication of where the forest started. Her eyes narrowed as she tried in vain to penetrate the blackness. There was no movement. Neither could she hear anything of significance to her non-jungle trained ears.

Her father had made a makeshift wooden table on which he had worked. Jane now carefully removed his papers from this and turned it up on its side, dragging it against the open door of the hut. The indians have no use for doors because the idea of private property is a strange concept to them. At least, felt Jane, the table would form some protection against any inquisitive animal which happened to wander through the village that night.

She then nibbled a bar of chocolate from her haversack and, turning the wick of the lamp down low, climbed into her father's sleeping bag, checking first for any insect or snake that might have decided to investigate its potential warmth.

She placed her Express rifle by her side and, using some packing cases to support her head, quickly fell into an uncomfortable semi-doze.

The sun, shining through the space between the table and the top of the hut doorway, awoke her as its fierce rays slanted across her face. She blinked rapidly and looked around the interior of the hut with incomprehension for nearly half a minute before her memory returned. She reached out a hurried hand and caught the stock of her rifle. It gave her some assurance and she breathed deeply in a half sigh.

Climbing out of the now stifling sleeping-bag she went to the hut doorway, pushed aside the upturned table and stepped out.

The sun was already high in the sky and she experienced a pang of annoyance at having slept so late.

A quick glance around the surrounding huts showed that the village remained deserted. Nothing stirred. No, not quite. Two wild deer stood hesitantly on one side of the clearing, nervously tugging at mouthfuls of the long reed-like *sapé* grass. Had the villagers been near, the deers would never have ventured even to the edge of the clearing, away from the protection of the forest.

Jane bit her lip and returned to the interior of the hut to pick up her rifle and some biscuits which she nibbled thoughtfully as she made her way to the rocky clearing where a rivulet cascaded its way through the rocks. She knelt by its side and splashed the cold, refreshing water on her face. Then she filled her water bottle and drank long and deeply.

Her fear of the night had vanished; the inexplicable terror was gone and she smiled ruefully at what she now considered a piece of emotional stupidity.

Fear always seems to be made better by the bright morning sun.

But fear aside, the situation was perplexing and Jane could offer no explanations for the deserted village, the vanished villagers or the disappearance of her father.

She sat by the side of the gushing rivulet trying to fathom some reasonable explanation for the hurried departure of her father and the indians. But no explanation was forthcoming. She sighed again in her perplexity. There was only one thing to do. Captain Orlando Villas would be returning maybe later that day or, at least, on the morrow. Perhaps he would be able to solve the mystery.

Jane was not given to flights of fancy and she did not doubt that there was some logical explanation to the situation. However, it was going to be tedious awaiting the return of the *Falcão*.

She stood up and began to wander around the village clearing. It crossed her mind that perhaps the villagers had left some evidence as to which direction they had taken.

To one side of the clearing she came upon a peculiar sight. It was almost as if a new pathway had been cut through the forest. There, through the middle of dense waving undergrowth, of swaying *sapé* grass, and thickly growing bushes, was a pathway perhaps some twenty feet in width which ran clearly through the jungle and vanished over the rocky hillocks some distance away. Jane frowned. It was certainly a fresh path for it had not been cut when she had previously been at the village. Perhaps the Trumái had cut it for some purpose such as establishing a new trackway to maintain contact with an interior tribe. But knowing the indian's social customs as she did, Jane felt that explanation hardly likely. And why build a path twenty feet wide?

'Curiouser and curiouser,' she smiled as she quoted *Alice*

*in Wonderland* under her breath. 'This seems a day full of mysteries.'

The pathway was extremely well cut, the grass was short, so short that it was a mere dried stubble almost flush with the hard sunbaked earth. Bushes and other vegetation had disappeared but the trees were left like tall posts along its wide belt.

She shook her head slowly and was turning away when a flash of white along the path caused her to blink and turn. Screwing up her eyes she could see that the fierce rays of the sun were reflecting on some object or objects almost hidden by a cluster of trees about a hundred yards along the track.

Tucking her rifle under her arm she walked towards the flashing object.

As she drew nearer she could discern a large pile of something that was white and, in the glinting rays of the sun, the shiny whiteness was causing a myriad of flashes and dancing lights to play over the pile.

One hand shading her eyes, Jane moved closer.

She was still some distance away when a feeling of amazement began to grow in her. The pile became visible. It was a pile of bones . . . and as she moved closer she realised, with a shudder, they were human bones.

She stood gazing on the pile opened mouthed. It was a neat pile; a pile that had been neatly stacked. A pile which must contain over fifty skeletons. But the bones were so white, so new . . . Jane stepped forward; she suddenly realised that her mouth was dry, that her heart was beating a rapid tattoo, the blood singing in her ears. Mechanically she looked at the bones, the row of skulls peering at her with sightless eyes. They were small skeletons. Somehow, in a detached way, the anthropologist part of her mind registered that they were skeletons of non-Europeans; the skull shape, the thick-set bone structure. But why were they so new . . . so neatly piled?

Indian skeletons. Of that there was no doubt. But . . . one skeleton caught her trained eye, now functioning completely automatically. This was definitely a European skull, even the dental care of the teeth marked it out as

European. Something flashed about its neck and Jane bent forward to examine it.

Icy hands started to clutch at her heart as she saw a gold locket; a small round gold locket on a chain. A locket which had belonged to her mother and which, after her mother's death, her father had always worn about his neck.

She experienced falling from a great height towards a still pool of black water as the realisation hammered into her mind.

This was her father's skeleton!

These were the skeletons of the missing villagers!

Then she hit the black water. It was ice cold and engulfed her completely.

How long she lay senseless before the gruesome pile she did not know. Her head was pounding and her tongue was dry and rasping in a cracked and swollen mouth. Her body felt cold and shivering while her face was flaming with surging hot blood.

She moaned.

A sudden rustling in the undergrowth forced her to shake her head to try to clear it and reached out for the protection of her rifle.

It seemed several minutes while she crouched blinking around at the surrounding forest.

Nothing stirred. A tiny voice at the back of her frantically heaving mind told her that perhaps it had been some animal scuttling away into the safety of the interior of the woods.

She climbed unsteadily to her feet and, in a daze, staggered back towards the village.

She tried to still the torrent of thoughts that rushed through her mind and, in her state of shock, partially succeeded. She went to her father's hut, moving almost automatically, and found some aspirin. She swallowed these with large gulps of water and then sat trying to regain control over her quivering limbs.

It was some time before she felt sufficiently recovered to stand up and return along the path to the pile of grisly relics. Setting her face in harsh lines she went straight to the skeleton with the locket and carefully removed the piece of jewellery. There was no question that this was her father's locket. Then, fighting down a nausea, she looked carefully at the teeth of the skeleton. She knew her father had recently had two fillings in his back teeth. Sure enough, two back teeth in the skeleton's jawbone contained fillings.

She stepped back from the pile of bones and surveyed them in horror.

How had the indians and her father died? Of what had they died? How could the bodies decompose so quickly, leaving only skeletons. According to Captain Villas her father had been alive and well only two weeks ago. Why were the skeletons so new, so bright, so shiny as if . . . the nausea welled in her stomach . . . as if some animal had stripped clean the bones? Ridiculous thought! Perhaps some awful epidemic had overtaken the village? Perhaps the survivors had burnt the bodies in a mass grave leaving only the skeletons? But if that were so, where were the signs of that fire? Why weren't the bones black and charred?

The torrent of unanswered questions poured into her mind.

She reached out a hand as if to prevent herself from falling and even staggered a step or two before regaining her balance.

Realising the futility of fainting again, she bent her head forward to aid the circulation and began to breath deeply.

The danger of fainting mastered, she retraced her steps back to the village.

She reached the stream and sat down, realising as she did so that she had dropped her rifle by the skeletons in her moment of weakness. She ought to return to get it. No, she could not face going back there for awhile.

She sat silent and still for perhaps half an hour before her body was suddenly overtaken by wave after wave of shivering and then tears sprang to her eyes and a gurgling laughter took over, mishaping her mouth and face. It was nearly an hour later when the hysteria subsided, leaving her totally exhausted. She fell into an uneasy but exhausted sleep where she lay.

When she came to, for it was hardly awakening from a sleep in the true sense, she felt the emotion was drained out of her being. She felt cold and detached. Survival was a prime motive and hunger forced her to her feet and made her trace her footsteps towards her father's hut to get some biscuits.

She hesitated on the threshold of the hut. Some sense warned her that the hut was not as she had left it. She saw the reason almost at once. The stack of provisions had been toppled from their shelves, a bag of sugar lay spilled upon the floor; several cans of food had been dented and a pack of biscuits had been ripped open and half of them consumed.

As she stood there, she suddenly caught a movement in the gloom at the back of the hut.

Her hand made an automatic reach before, with a chilling coldness, Jane Sewell realised that she had left her rifle lying in front of the grisly pile of skeletons and that her father's rifle had been stacked by her at the back of the hut.

## CHAPTER FOUR

Jane Sewell stood like a statue.

She felt cold and emotionless; all the emotion seemed to have been drained from her slim frame by the trauma of hysteria. Now she realised that she did not feel alarm at the lurking shadow, nor at the fact that she was weaponless. All she felt was a growing curiosity.

'Who's there?' she demanded.

There was no reply and she repeated the question, first in Portuguese and then in the Xingu indian language.

There was still no answer.

She moved slowly forward and, as she did so, her eye caught sight of her father's walking stick lying near the hut entrance. She made a swoop for it and while she was in the act of grasping its thin ebony handle, a small shadow detached itself from the gloom, dodged past her and leapt away behind the nearby huts. Grasping the stick, Jane turned and followed.

She saw the back of a small indian boy dodging behind a hut on the far side of the village.

'Stop!' she cried. 'I mean you no harm. Come back!'

She halted when she realised that pursuit was useless. She caught a glimpse of a small face peering at her in consternation around the edges of a hut.

She forced a smile.

'Come here. I will not hurt you. I am a friend.'

But the small face disappeared as soon as she took a step forward.

Jane frowned in annoyance.

Who was the boy? He could only be about ten years old or thereabouts. If he were one of the village children he might be able to explain what had happened. Some explanation was needed. The boy was certainly scared and usually the indians were not scared of strangers. They were a simple people by lived by a simple code of hospitality and trusted all strangers for they had not yet encountered the machinations and deceptions of the white man. It was therefore peculiar that an indian should behave as if he were scared of a stranger.

How could she entice the boy back?

Out of the corner of her eye she saw the boy's face still observing her round the side of the hut. It came to her suddenly that the boy was probably hungry, she had disturbed him in the act of raiding the food provisions in her father's hut. And it also dawned on her at the same time that she was extremely hungry herself.

She returned to the hut, entered and scoured the shelves in search of food. There was a large tin of stewed steak and a couple of tins of baked beans. She opened them and mixed them into a mash in a saucepan. She then picked up the primus stove, went outside the hut and set it up. Soon the mess of beans and steak were simmering in the pan. The boy had drawn closer. Jane went back into the hut, took a couple of plates and two spoons and a packet of plain biscuits and sat herself before the primus stove. It was not exactly a menu prescribed by the Ritz-Carlton but it was food. Carefully she spooned some of the mess into a plate, added a couple of biscuits and a spoon and placed it on a rock on the far side of the primus stove, a little way from her.

'If you are hungry,' she called in Xingu, 'you are welcome to eat.'

Then, entirely ignoring the boy, she helped herself to her own share and commenced to eat.

After a while she became aware that the figure of the small boy had detached itself from the hut and had taken several hesitant paces towards the steaming plate of food. The eyes of the little boy were black and round, his mouth enclosed a thumb which he sucked on solemnly, and his expression was one of fixed intensity on the tantalising aspect of hot food. Jane examined him under lowered lids. He was, indeed, about ten years old and certainly looked as if he might belong to the Trumái tribe. His body was lithe and coppery and he wore his blue-black hair cut off at a uniform length just below his ears. He wore the traditional *api* penis sheath but no ornamentation.

Twice the boy took a hesitant step forward and then cast anxious, round eyes glance at the girl. Jane continued her own eating and fixed her eyes firmly on her plate. It was not long before she heard the rasping of a spoon on the plate and the gasping breath of the young boy as he shovelled the food into his mouth.

She waited a while and then raised her eyes to watch the boy, mouth working, cheeks bulging, ramming the food home more quickly than he could swallow it. Jane reached forward and poured a tin mug of water and held it out towards the boy. He stopped eating, his eyes never ceased watching her face.

She smiled and nodded towards the mug.

'Are you thirsty?' she asked in Xingu.

The boy continued to look at her face and then, almost imperceptibly, nodded.

'Drink then,' said Jane.

The boy came cautiously forward and reached out, took the mug and drained off the contents in one swallow. Jane smilingly refilled the mug. She noticed the peculiar tenseness of the child. It seemed that every muscle of his body was taut with expectation and any little noise would cause it to jerk, his eyes to sweep wildly round for danger, his lips to quiver. It seemed that the child had not eaten in a long time and Jane let him eat and drink his fill.

'What name do they call you?' she asked, after he had finished and sat looking up at her with his large solemn eyes.

He made no reply.

Jane gave an encouraging smile and asked the question again.

The child frowned, half opened his mouth and made an inarticulate hissing sound through puckered lips. Two large tears sprang into the child's eyes and he opened his mouth wide, baring his teeth and making terrible grunting noises.

Jane was momentarily startled.

'You poor thing,' she cried suddenly. 'You're mute. You can't speak. But you can hear, can't you?' She resorted to Xingu again. 'Are you from this village? You can understand me, can't you?'

The child let the tears cascade down his cheeks and seemed to nod unhappily.

'You are from this village?' asked Jane once more to make certain.

The child nodded again.

'What happened? Where is everyone?'

At the question the child's face seemed to crumble, a howl of anguish came from his gaping mouth and sob upon sob racked his body. Jane reached out and caught the child in her arms. The small boy clung to her fiercely, his head buried against her neck. She could feel the hot tears springing from his eyes, saturating her blouse, feel his tense little body racked by his anguish.

Automatically she began to talk to him gently and to rock to and fro to comfort him.

'Poor little one,' she murmured in English, 'do you know what happened here. Did you see it? Is that why you are sobbing? Or were you playing in the forest and came back to find the village deserted and only you were left in the frightening forest?'

It was fairly dark when the child's sobs had died away.

Jane peered at the growing twilight.

'A fine pair we are,' she said, trying to put a feeling of *bonhomie* into her voice. 'Here we are spending the day in tears when we should be doing something. Well, I should think that old Martinez and the *Falcāo* should be coming down river fairly soon now. Maybe tomorrow. We'll just have to wait so we might as well get some rest, eh?'

Gently she untangled the boy from her and stood up. The child still clung fiercely to her arm.

'We must sleep now,' she told him in Xingu, 'for tomorrow we shall go on a long boat journey . . .'

She turned towards the hut but was halted abruptly by the cough of a nearby cat, perhaps a jaguar, which caused her to tense and the little boy at her side to give a half stifled whimper of fear.

She went into the hut to find her father's rifle. It was the first time she had really looked at it and as she did so she could not stifle a cry of surprise. Every wooden part of the rifle had vanished. She bent towards it and examined it carefully. The leather straps and the wooden butt were no longer fixed to the metal barrel or trigger mechanism. It was as if someone had unscrewed them. She rummaged around in the hut but could not find them. Why had her father unscrewed them?

'Damn,' she suddenly cried loudly.

Her father's rifle was useless and her own .303 Express was still lying where she had dropped it by the pile of skeletons. She must have some form of protection for the coming night. She looked quickly at the sky, it was that final moment now, the turning point between twilight and darkness. She turned to the oil lamp and lit it.

'Listen, little one,' she told the boy, 'I have to go on a little walk to the forest to fetch something. Will you wait here for me? The lamp is burning brightly and there is no reason for you to be afraid now.'

The boy firmly shook his head and clung more tightly to her hand.

'Oh, very well,' she lapsed into English and then, in an attempt to bolster her spirits, added ruefully, I can see this might develop into a problem later'.

Leaving the oil lamp burning in the hut, she picked up

an electric pocket torch and, with the boy hanging onto her, crossed the deserted village square. By the time she came to the start of the great newly cut pathway it was totally dark and she began to move slowly and carefully along it, the pocket torch describing a small arc of light before her and more than once she had to halt to let some nocturnal creature slither swiftly out of her path. Once or twice a large snake paused and reared its head, tiny bead like eyes glaring balefully at her, and then the head went down and the great coils undulated into the blackness.

There was no moon and even the stars were obscured by great black billowing clouds. She nearly missed the gruesome pile of bones and only a glint of white, caught in the angle of her torch, made her pause and sweep the beam up across the neatly stacked remains. At the sight of them, the small boy cried in terror and she gently reassured him that there was nothing to fear.

It took some moments of searching before she came across her rifle.

As she bent to pick it up she suddenly paused and stood back in bewilderment.

Carefully, she let the beam of the torch play along the metal barrel, over the metal trigger mechanism to the stock . . . she fought down a cry of surprise. Every wooden part of the rifle, like her father's, had vanished. She stared in horrified disbelief.

Abruptly she was aware of a high pitched sound, almost a tinkling sound like tiny silvery bells. No sooner did she raise her head in a listening attitude than the sound ceased. There was a sudden rustling from the surrounding undergrowth.

The next thing she knew was that she was running, dragging the small boy along by one arm, wildly waving her torch over the ground before her. She ran uncaring of the nocturnal dangers of the pathway, her eyes were fixed towards the faint shadows cast by the indian huts.

She did not stop running until she was bathing in the light of the oil lamp in her father's hut; had swung the table across the mouth of the hut and was rummaging through her father's belongings for some kind of weapon –

any weapon – by which to defend herself. She was in luck for, in a corner of her father's chest, she found his old .38 revolver. It was a heavy Smith and Wesson Centennial Airweight which he used to carry more as a status symbol than for any practical reason. The .38 was no earthly good for stopping a jaguar or any other of the terrors of the jungle but now, at least, it gave Jane some confidence.

She sat on the sleeping bag, the small boy curled up at her side, the revolver gripped in one hand. Sleep did not come to her. It was not until the first white fingers of dawn began to creep into the eastern sky that her tired eye lids closed.

It was perhaps two hours later when the shrill shrieking of Martinez' klaxon horn heralded the approach of the old *Falcão* downriver.


## CHAPTER FIVE

Jane Sewell shook the young indian awake with an urgency which caused the boy to spring up, eyes wide in terror, body braced to encounter some terrifying danger.

Jane reached out a contrite hand to pacify his trembling limbs.

'I'm sorry. There's nothing to fear. It's only Martinez and the *Falcão* returning.'

As if to confirm her words, the three shrill blasts of the *Falcão*'s steam whistle came again.

Jane grabbed her haversack and thrust a few things into it, including some of her father's papers. Then, pushing the .38 revolver into her waistband, she took the young boy by the hand and set off at a quick trot through the village and along the pathway which led to the river. The boy trotted along confidently at her side, his hand tightly in hers, leaving all the decisions to her. The lines of strain and tension had almost disappeared from his face.

The adaptability of childhood, mused Jane. But even she was finding some relief to the perplexing mystery. The steam whistle of the old *Falcão* was a reassuring sound, something familiar in the nightmare world into which she had plunged. She found herself looking forward to seeing the punctilious Captain Villas of the *prefeitos* and leaving the mystery to him to solve; she found herself evolving a childlike belief in the ability of the policeman to provide some plausible reason for the horrific situation.

It was not long before they came to the wooden jetty which was so grandly known as Ponto Paulo. There was her baggage still piled neatly on the jetty awaiting collection. She sat the young boy on the baggage while she paced up and down waiting for the *Falcão* to round the bend in the river.

It was a few moments before it did so, careering wildly past the shallows. It seemed as if the helmsman had difficulty in controlling the steam boat.

As Jane's eyes took in the boat, which seemed to wallow from side to side like some sick whale, she knew instinctively that something was wrong.

There was no one on deck, although she could just discern a figure in the wheelhouse.

The foam was churning under the boat's stern and it seemed that it was heading down river at full speed.

For a second or so Jane thought that Martinez was going to pass by and she waved her arms and shouted.

The *Falcão* suddenly swerved crazily in midstream, then it appeared that the helmsman swung the wheel around and the old steamboat turned sluggishly in her own length and came straight for the wooden jetty, its engines still racing.

Jane leapt for the bank crying at the same time to the boy to get to safety.

A moment later the bows of the boat had smashed through the wooden jetty and buried themselves in the mud of the river bank. The boat was stuck fast, its whole bulk shuddering with the vibration of its engines; quivering like a fish which had just been landed.

Jane lay for a second where she had fallen, her breath completely knocked out of her. The boy, more nimble, rose to his feet and rushed to her side trying to pull her upwards, his face was distorted in anxiety and a tiny whimpering sound came from his mouth.

Gradually Jane sat up and laid a reassuring hand on the boy's shoulder.

'It's all right, little one,' she said gently. 'It's all right.'

The boy seemed half reassured and clung to her hand.

Jane looked at the quivering bulk of the *Falcão* and bit her lip. There was no sign of anyone moving aboard.

'Hello!' she cried.

Only the wild threshing of the *Falcão*'s propellers answered her and even those were slowly silenced as the old boat settled down in the mud and began to bury the props, leaving the protesting whine of the engine itself.

Jane rose to her feet, disengaged the boy's hand and pointed to the ground.

'Stay here. I will see what is wrong.'

The boy nodded a little unwillingly.

Jane clambered over the remains of the wooden jetty and swung herself aboard the boat. She stood hesitantly, looking along the deserted deck.

'Commandante Martinez? Captain Villas?'

There was no answer. Jane experienced a feeling of dreadful familiarity.

She walked slowly to the wheel house. Through the dirty glass she could see the figure of old Martinez slumped over his wheel.

'Commandante . . .?' Jane opened the door.

She was not sure what happened next. She was merely aware that the far door of the wheelhouse was hanging crazily off its hinges, torn off in the crash. She was also aware of seeing something . . . a something indefinable . . . a reddish black mass, like a pancake, a mass which pulsated and which, as she opened the wheelhouse door, seemed to scuttle out of the other. It took place in a split second and Jane even doubted whether she had seen anything at all . . . perhaps it had been a shadow cast by the flickering sunlight through the trees which bespeckled the boat in tiny shadows.

'Commandante Martinez,' she began again.

Then she had to stop the scream that welled in her throat.

Martinez was slumped over the wheel. His hands still

grasped it, grasped it with such fierceness that the skin was taut enough for the bones of his knuckles to almost pierce through. His eyes were still wide open and on his face was frozen an expression of hideous anguish. His lips had been so chewed that they were lacerated and bloody. But the face was a death mask.

It was then that Jane noticed the lower half of his body. Nausea swept in waves through her body and she had to turn away to give vent to her feelings.

The bottom of Martinez' legs appeared to have been eaten away. The flesh was mangled and bloody and in some places the bones stood through glistening white. Only some fierce determination had kept the old man at the wheel of his beloved *Falcão* until he died where he stood.

Jane raised her head from between her knees and was aware that the young boy, his face full of concern, was trying to climb aboard.

'Stay there!' she commanded. 'It's all right but stay there!'

The boy hesitated and she repeated the order. The boy had had enough shocks without seeing the grisly sight of the river boat captain.

Softly she closed the wheelhouse door on its terrible occupant.

But where was Captain Villas? Where were Martinez' two indian hands?

She wiped her clammy face, bathed in a cold sweat, with a handkerchief and took several deep breaths.

A low moan caused her to wheel round and peer fearfully towards the back of the boat.

A cabin door was slowly opening. Jane dropped her hand to the .38. The figure of a man fell through the door and collapsed onto the deck. He was making whimpering noises like some animal in pain. His face, hands and legs were a mass of red raw mangled flesh. Jane felt her stomach heaving again at the terrible sight. With a catch of her breath she recognised the shredded uniform that the man wore.

'Captain Villas!'

The man had collapsed on his face.

Fighting down her nausea, she hurried to his side and somehow managed to get him over on his back. The face was horrible to behold. It was a mass of mutilated flesh, caked with blood, which bore no resemblance to a human face at all. One eye blinked out, focusing on the girl.

Something moved within the mess of blood . . . a mouth.

'Sen . . . senhorinha . . .'

The word was a mere breath.

'Captain Villas . . . what happened?'

Bubbles of blood spurted from the hole in the face. Villas' voice sounded as if it were speaking under water.

'For . . . formiga . . .'

A sudden spasm went through the mutilated body and then it was still. Jane rose and stepped away from the dead man, a thousand thoughts pouring in a torrent through her head.

*Formiga.* Jane shook her head in bewilderment. What was Villas trying to say? *Formiga* was the Portuguese word for ants. Why should Villas talk of ants with his dying breath? Perhaps he had not finished the word. Perhaps he was trying to say *formigamento* which would have meant 'burning' or 'itching', which might have described how he felt in his terribly mutilated condition.

She suddenly noticed that the indian boy was trying to attract her attention from the bank. He was jumping up and down and pointing to the boat. She realised that the deck was tilting dangerously beneath her feet. The old river boat was heeling over in the mud.

A cold determination took over. Fighting her distaste, she bent over the dead police captain and unbuckled his cartridge belt and threw it onto the bank. Then she opened the cabin door and peered in. She knew that Villas carried a rifle and she realised that she needed it if she was going to be left alone in the jungle without a means of getting back to Morená except her own two feet. The rifle was lying on the floor of the cabin just inside the door.

She bent down and even as her fingers closed on the stock of the rifle, the boat gave a sudden lurch and heeled over ten degrees. Jane pushed herself quickly out of the cabin, ignoring the inert mass of Villas' body, and climbed on to the side of the boat. Then she crawled along to the bows and managed to leap off onto the embankment.

The boy ran towards her his mouth moving, and flung his arms around her waist in a tight embrace.

Absently, she patted his head, unwound his arms and told him to stay still while she recovered Villas' cartridge belt. She checked the rifle to make sure she knew how to work it and that it was loaded. Then she sat down and pulled out some chocolate for the boy to eat. She realised that it was midmorning and they had not eaten or drunk anything since the night before. Even so, after what she had seen on the *Falcão*, she could not bring herself to touch anything.

There were important things to think of now. How was she going to get back to Morená?

A sucking-like noise, the whine of a racing engine and a crashing of metal and wood heralded the final lurch of the old *Falcão*. The old river boat now lay completely on its side, one part of it fully submerged in the water. Its one solitary lifeboat lay splintered into matchwood beneath it, so there was no hope of using that to get downriver.

Jane sat for a moment biting her nails and trying to think of her next step. Her only hope lay in taking the indian boy and heading down river in the direction of Morená, although she knew that she would never be able to reach the town on her own. Nevertheless, along the river banks there would be some native settlements and perhaps she would be able to strike one of the large plantations that were sparsely dotted about.

She turned to the boy who was ravenously devouring the chocolate bar which she had given him.

'We've a long journey ahead of us, little one,' she told him in Xingu. 'So first we will have to go back to the village and collect all the food we can find.'

The boy nodded.

Hitching the rifle over her shoulder, along with her haversack, Jane took the boy by the hand and turned back towards the village.

# CHAPTER SIX

Fifteen thousand feet above, in the crisp azure sky, Hugo Martin looked down at the green carpet of the tree tops of the tropical rain forest with anxiety creasing his forehead. He gently pushed the joystick of his twin engined Merlin forward to increase his airspeed and drew his anxious gaze back to the bank of instruments and dials before him. For the third time in the last five minutes he cursed the aging Merlin under his breath. All the dials, petrol and oil gauges, gave reassuring readings but the Merlin was behaving sluggishly and the engines kept going into a paroxysm of stuttering and coughing. If the petrol gauges were not holding steadily on a quarter full, Hugo would have sworn the tanks were dangerously empty.

For two months now Hugo had been telling his employer that the Swearingen SA-26T Merlin II, to give it its full designation, was coming to her last days. The fact was that the aircraft should have been scrapped years ago. The Merlin, a cabin cruiser which could hold six passengers as well as a pilot and co-pilot, had once been the last word in light aircraft when they started to roll from the production line in April, 1965. They were fine aircraft with a good cruising speed of 280 m.p.h., a ceiling of 30,000 feet and a range of 1,340 miles. That was why a number of big estate owners, such as José Joaquin de Silva Xavier, for whom Hugo flew, had invested in them. It had once been the boast of the Merlin that it could climb on one of its Pratt and Whitney turboprops with a full load. But now the American aeroplane was old and worn.

Hugo had realised the fraility of the old craft almost as soon as he went to work on Senhor Xavier's plantation some two years before. He had been employed by Senhor Xavier as a crop-dusting pilot and also to ferry supplies and people between the plantation and Moraná or even as far as Cuiaba, the provincial capital. It was a good job and well paid. Hugo had been grateful to Xavier, for jobs for

35

ex-fighter pilots demobbed from the United States Air Force were few and far between.

The Merlin's portside engine coughed again and Hugo dipped his nose to keep the airspeed up. If only Senhor Xavier had spent more money on maintenance or had bought a new machine . . .

The portside engine heaved a sigh and suddenly its rhythmic beat halted. Its prop swung idly for a moment and then stopped its rotation.

Automatically, Hugo leant forward and flicked off the port engine switch. He bit his lip as his eyes once more scanned his instruments. His instinct told him that no petrol was getting through to the engine, contrary to what his gauges told him.

The port engine petrol gauge needle stood defiantly at a quarter full.

He swore.

The needle should have read 'zero' after he had switched off.

He reached forward and tapped the dial. The needle did not even tremble.

'Okay, baby,' crooned Hugo, caressing the joystick, 'you could once climb with a full load on one engine, well let's see you take me home with one engine.'

He looked around the sky and then at the ground, seeking a landmark. Just under his starboard wing was the silvery ribbon of the River Xingu, threading its careful way between banks of tall trees. The plantation of Senhor José Joaquin de Silva Xavier was a good thirty miles away on the port side.

Hugo banked the aircraft a little and gently brought it round to fall off towards the port. He had hardly done so when the starboard engine coughed, spluttered, failed, picked up, failed again and was silent.

The old Merlin, both engines out, began its whispering glide towards the trees.

A coldness seized Hugo, although he kept his body relaxed in his seat.

'Now, baby,' he said, reproachfully, 'that's no way to treat a guy.' He eased the port rudder and slowly slewed the aircraft round to starboard, his eyes straining to pick up the silvery ribbon of the Xingu. His only hope of getting down in one piece was to come down in the river, there was no way he was going to survive if his 'plane pancaked into the trees.

The air was chattering past the cockpit now as the Merlin began to increase its downward glide. He kept bringing the nose up to decrease his airspeed and, as an additional brake, he put his flaps full on.

He managed to line up with the river, hoping that when he finally came down he would come down upon a straight stretch.

The green vegetation seemed to rush towards him. Both hands on the stick he pushed the nose towards the silvery ribbon which, as it came to meet him, turned blue and then muddy-brown.

'This is it, baby,' he breathed, 'You can make it now . . . you can make it.'

But even as he spoke he knew that he was wrong. His speed was too fast, he was going to overshoot the river where it suddenly lurched round a promontory.

The old Merlin shot across the river at an angle, causing a cascade of spray to fly fifty feet into the air, and with a screaming of metal and snapping of wood, the aircraft rushed up the bank of the river and smashed a pathway into the jungle.

For about thirty seconds after the twisted mess came to a standstill there was perfect silence in the jungle. Then the angry chatter of animals rose like a chorus all around.

Jane Sewell paused as she heard the swish of the aeroplane as it slid out of the sky. She saw the smack of its belly landing, saw its race across the surface of the river a quarter of a mile away from where she and the boy stood, and, finally, saw it disappear into a violence of flying debris in among the trees. For a moment she stood stock still, appalled by the unexpectedness and violence of the crash.

She swayed for a moment, placing both hands to her head, convinced that she was losing her mind. Since she had disembarked from the *Falcão* two days before it seemed

37

that she had entered a nightmare world, a world of inexplicable and horrifying events, a world that she could not begin to come to terms with.

She gave a hysterical giggle.

There was a sharp tug on her sleeve. The indian boy gazed up at her, his dark eyes wide with concern.

Jane drew herself together. The child trusted and relied on her. It was her duty to get them both to a point of civilisation. She looked upriver to where a large cloud of dust was settling in the area in which the aircraft had disappeared.

'Come on,' she suddenly said firmly, taking the child by the hand. 'We better see if there are any survivors . . . we might be able to help.'

It took some time before they came upon the wrecked Merlin. Jane and the boy followed a narrow path along the river's edge but the path was overgrown in places and sometimes disappeared altogether where the embankment had been undermined by the river and fallen away. Bushes and undergrowth seemed to deliberately impede their progress and twice Jane started as some animal scuttled resentfully out of her path. It was half an hour before she came upon the pathway which the aircraft had mown into the forest.

She saw that the aircraft had been travelling at some speed. For about three hundred yards distance it had smashed vegetation and small trees before it. Incredibly she observed that the fuselage of the 'plane had passed between the larger trees, merely encountering on its headlong rush small saplings and bushes which had soon been uprooted. The wings had been ripped off but the fuselage had carried on it one piece until, as it slowed down, it had finally grazed into a tree which had sheered one side of it away.

Jane motioned the boy to remain where he was while she approached the wreck. Some distant warning clamoured in the back of her mind that crashed aircraft usually burst into flames and made her pause. But there was no sign of fire. She did not know that the fuel tanks had been empty and there was therefore no danger of fire at all.

As she approached through the litter of the machine

which strewed the ground, she noticed what she thought to be a bundle of clothing. Then she realised that it was the body of a man, the pilot, lying on his back near the splintered cabin of the aircraft. She could not tell whether he had been thrown clear or had climbed out of the aircraft by himself before he had collapsed.

She was about to start towards him when she stopped in her tracks.

A reddy-black mass seemed to cover the prone pilot's chest. Red highlights flickered in the light of the sun that crept through the trees. It seemed as if the mass was pulsating.

What was it? Some animal? A giant spider? The thoughts flashed through her mind.

Not quite knowing what she was doing, Jane unhitched her rifle from her shoulder, pushed the bolt forward to send a round into the breech and fired a shot into the air.

The effect was unexpected.

The pulsating mass seemed to scuttle away from the man's chest, moving with an irregular movement, changing shape from a circle to an oval to an oblong, almost flowing across the clearing and disappearing into the jungle undergrowth. Jane had never seen anything like it. It looked like no animal she could name. But she could not spare any more thought to the matter.

She walked quickly to the prostrate form and knelt down. The pilot was a young man, perhaps in his early thirties, tall with fair hair and bronzed finely chiselled features. There was an ugly bruise over one temple and several minor abrasions. He was breathing and Jane swiftly ran her hands over his legs and arms. As far as she could tell there were no bones broken.

She turned and waved the indian boy to come closer. With strange animals about it were best if they kept together. She took her water bottle and forced some of the liquid between the unconscious man's lips.

Hugo Martin thought that he was drowning. Trapped in the cabin of his Merlin as it hit the river, he thought the aircraft was sinking into the depths of its muddy bottom, saw the water spilling over the cockpit and trickling in.

Now the water was filling up the cockpit as he fought to escape; relentlessly it filled and was even now trickling into his mouth and throat.

He opened his mouth to cry out and waved his hands in a vain effort to push back the water.

'It's all right,' said a voice, soft and reassuring. 'It's all right. You're safe now.'

Hugo opened his eyes and saw a girl bending over him with a water bottle. He blinked and tried to sit up.

A terrific weight in his head forced him back with a groan. He became conscious of his body, a veritable sack of throbbing pain.

'What happened?' he asked, knowing it was a ridiculous question before he had finished asking it.

The girl smiled.

'You crashed. But you're all right.'

Hugo swallowed some more water.

With a groan he forced himself into a sitting position. His head had several steamhammers thundering away in it. He put his weight on his left arm and collapsed with an involuntary scream of agony. The girl helped him into a sitting position.

'It's not broken,' she said. 'It's probably a sprain.'

'I feel like death,' muttered Hugo.

The girl nodded sympathetically.

'Was there anyone else in the aircraft when you came down?'

Hugo shook his head.

'Just me.'

'I'll bandage that wrist of yours then,' returned the girl and began to rummage in her haversack bringing out some bandages which she wound tightly round his wrist. The throbbing pain was still there but he felt curiously eased.

'You haven't a couple of aspirin, have you?' he asked hopefully. 'I've a hell of a headache.'

He swallowed the two pills Jane gave him and lay back with his eyes closed for a moment.

Jane and the boy wandered round the wreckage but there was nothing to salvage.

40

When they returned they found the pilot looking at them with a painful and puzzled smile.

'Who are you?'

She told him.

'My name is Hugo Martin,' he said. 'American. You sound as if you're English?'

'I am,' she confirmed.

'Who's the boy?'

'He comes from a Trumái village. I don't know his name. He's mute.'

She paused.

'Do you think you can walk for a while?'

Hugo grimaced.

'I can try. Why?'

'It's nearly a mile to the Trumái village and I reckon there will be a better shelter there than here tonight.'

He nodded and, with her aid, climbed to his feet. For a moment he swayed unsteadily and then regained his balance and tried a few experimental steps.

'I'm okay, I guess, apart from my wrist and head. I'm afraid you'll have to give me a hand though. Is your camp at this village?'

Jane thought it better not to complicate things and nodded. She supported one side of the pilot while the boy held the other side and the three of them began a slow, laborious progress back to the deserted Trumái village.

It was some hours, due to their slow progress through the forest, before the trio arrived there by which time the shadows of twilight were swooping in across the trees.

Hugo was in a pretty poor way; the sweat poured from his face and his breath was tortured and agonised. He groaned with each slow step. Jane brought him finally to the hut which had been her father's and she and the boy carefully laid the pilot in the sleeping bag. As on previous nights, Jane lit the oil lamp and pushed the table across the entrance to the hut. Then she and the boy bedded down in the opposite corner to Hugo, Jane sleeping with her hand close to her rifle.

It was an unpleasant, exhausting night for her. The boy quickly fell into a deep, seemingly peaceful sleep. But Jane lay awake for many hours listening to the laboured, ster-torous breathing of the American pilot, watching him toss and turn in a fever of painful sleep. Towards morning he gradually became calmer, his breathing more regular as his fever abated.

Then Jane, too, finally succumbed to a sleep born of sheer exhaustion; a sleep which, however, was haunted by strange animals, dancing skeletons, and the sight of old Martinez holding the wheel of the *Falcão* in his death grip, eyes wide and staring, a bizarre figure which turned, in the dream, into the figure of her own father. And when she jerked awake, one hand outstretched towards him, the sun was high in the sky and shining with a bright intensity into the hut.

## CHAPTER SEVEN

José Joaquin de Silva Xavier was worried.

He paced up and down the floor of his study while, in a corner, his plantation manager, Juan Lopez, fiddled irrit-ably with the knobs of the radio-telephone set. Finally, the swarthy faced Lopez turned and hunched his shoulders in a gesture of hopelessness.

'It is no good, senhor. The static is drowning out all communication. I cannot understand it.'

Xavier was a small man in his late forties with a shock of curly silver hair carefully brushed into place so not a rebellious hair stood out of place. His body was that of a younger man, lean and suntanned and his expensive clothes sat well upon him. His eyes were dark brown, almost black, and they had an ability to look neutral while he was thinking but flashed with a myriad fires when his anger was aroused.

Xavier's grandfather had moved into the interior of the Matto Grosso many years before, had explored the upper regions of the Xingu and finally carved out an empire for himself not far from the river. The empire was an estate of 50,000 acres; a plantation that had produced rubber; tons of it each year, but that had been before 1910 when the rubber boom in Brazil ended and it was found cheaper to produce rubber in South East Asia. Once upon a time, Brazil had produced 600,000 metric tons of rubber but now its share of the world market had dropped to only one per cent of the world trade, some 12,000 to 14,000 metric tons a year.

The Xavier wealth had been founded on rubber and the plantation continued to produce a good output of the national trade in competition with the Japanese planters who owned estates in the Lower Amazon basin. But it was a difficult business, even a company like Ford Motors, who had started a 5,000 acre plantation in Pará, found themselves unable to compete for the small share of the market which was now Brazil's.

It had been Xavier's father who, in the 1930s, had changed the major production of the plantation from rubber to manganese and cotton. Now one hundred indians worked on the plantation with seasonal work, such as cotton-picking, swelling that number twofold.

The government of the Matto Grosso state, which administered the Xingu National Park, had left the Xavier plantation alone on condition that Xavier did not interfere with the local tribes and their customs or way of life.

José Joaquin de Silva Xavier solemnly gave his promise and continued to work the plantation as his grandfather and father had worked it before him. He was the *Senhor de baraco e cutelo*, a feudal lord, with power of life and death over all the indians on his estate. He was a proud man who never let it be forgot that he was descended from the José Joaquin de Silva Xavier who had led the first Brazilian uprising against the Portuguese colonial power in 1798.

But now Xavier was a worried man.

His pilot, Hugo Martin, was long overdue at the plantation. He should have arrived on the previous afternoon from Morená bearing mail and some supplies. He had not arrived and now Xavier was trying to contact Morená by radio-telephone, the plantation's only link with the outside world, to find out whether the American had taken off from the airport.

43

His plantation manager, a dark, handsome man of thirty, Juan Lopez, had been unable to raise Morená due to some peculiar static.

'It's no good, senhor,' repeated Lopez.

'Try again, Lopez,' urged Xavier. 'If the American has taken off and crashed then we must send out a search party?'

Xavier suddenly smashed a balled fist into the palm of his hand.

'*Deus nos*, God forbid that anything has happened! For a long time he has been telling me that the old 'plane needed to be scrapped. But it had served me for a long time . . . I am responsible.'

Lopez shrugged and turned back to the radio-telephone.

'You are not to be blamed. The Yanqui was a trained pilot and used to do all his own repairs. If he has crashed, it is not your fault, senhor.'

There was no love lost between Lopez and the American pilot. In a distorted way, Lopez saw Hugo Martin as a rival. Although he, Lopez, was the plantation manager and Hugo was only a pilot employed to ferry goods and to spray the crops when wanted, Lopez resented his presence on the estate. Especially, as it seemed, when Xavier treated the Yanqui – and Lopez used the word with bitterness – as a friend rather than his employee. It was a relationship that Lopez never ever enjoyed.

He switched his mind back to the machinery before him. It was strange this static that assailed his ears. There was no explanation as to what was causing it. It was certainly not the set, he had checked it thoroughly twice. True, they were now in the middle of the Matto Grosso summer, the dry season from May to September. It was a period of short days, transparent skies with the air agitated by fresh gusts of wind mainly from the south. The nights were long and cold. In such conditions there frequently occurred great electrical storms above the high sierras. Perhaps that electricity was causing the interference?

Lopez moved a tuning knob carefully and, for a second, caught a squeaky voice. He carefully adjusted the dials.

44

The voice was faint through the crackling and whistling of the static.

'Hello? Hello? Is that Mo61ená. Over?'

The voice vacillated and vanished and then came back on a stronger pitch.

'Moená here. Moená here. Your signal is faint. Can you read me? Over.'

Lopez turned up the volume.'

'Your signal is also faint, Moená. Strength five. Static interference. Can you read me?'

'Positive. Identify . . .'

There was a loud whistling.

Xavier reached for the microphone.

'Moená, this is Senhor Xavier. Xavier. Did my pilot, Hugo Martin, take off as scheduled from your airport?'

'. . . ená. Your pilot . . . affirmative . . . at 1300 hours yesterday, senhor. He should have arrived at your plantation at 14.50 hours. Is he . . .'

The set resounded with crackles and whistles.

Lopez sighed.

'It is no good, senhor. The static is some outside interference. We just can't get through.'

Xavier nodded and plucked at his lower lip.

'Nevertheless, Lopez, we have heard enough, *não e*? Hugo took off on schedule. That means he has crashed.'

He went to his desk and spread out a map of the area.

'His flight plan would probably be down river to Ponto Paulo before swinging inland towards the plantation. Lopez, send in Kanaraté. I want half a dozen men organised with food, water and a medical kit. We must start a search immediately.'

Kanaraté was an indian who had worked on the plantation for nearly thirty years and knew every pathway through the surrounding forests.

Lopez stood up with a begrudging look on his face.

'*Veja*,' he grunted the Portuguese slang of 'okay'.

José Joaquin de Silva Xavier bent his worried brow over the map.

'Really, I feel fine,' said Hugo Martin for the third time since he had awoken.

Jane Sewell repacked the thermometer with which she had been taking his temperature.

'Well, the fever seems to have disappeared all right,' she agreed. 'But how's the wrist?'

Hugo touched it with his right hand and winced slightly.

'Must be a sprain. It still aches a bit but it's okay. I guess I'll pull through but my body throbs like hell.'

'You're lucky to be alive,' said Jane.

'Too true. I've used up my quota of luck. First getting out of that death trap of a Merlin alive . . .'

Jane frowned. 'Merlin?' she interrupted.

'Yeah. The crate . . . the aircraft, that is, that I was flying.'

'I see.'

'Then you showing up out of nowhere to patch me up and bring me here,' Hugo gestured to the hut. 'We're in some kind of indian village, eh?'

'We are in a Trumái village near Ponto Paulo,' confirmed Jane. 'Ah, the coffee's ready now.'

She had been percolating some coffee in a pot on the primus stove while the indian boy had sat looking on in wide-eyed silence.

Hugo reached out his good hand for a cup.

'Ponto Paulo, eh?' he said, sipping at the steaming contents. 'I thought I was in that vicinity. I was trying to pancake . . . er, to make a belly landing on the river.'

'What was wrong?' asked the girl, handing another cup to the young boy who took it eagerly.

'The old crate – my aircraft – was just too old. Her instruments packed up on me and I ran out of gas without knowing. So I came down.'

He suddenly frowned.

'Say, it's kind of quiet here for an indian village, isn't it? What goes on?'

'The place is deserted. There is something mysterious and . . . and frightening here.'

Suddenly the nervous tension of the last few days began to bubble in her voice.

'They are gone, all gone, the people – my father. I was waiting for old Martinez and Captain Villas but they are dead . . .'

The words started to come out in a rush.

Hugo held up his good hand.

'Whoa, lady. Martinez and Villas I know. Dead, you say? The village deserted? You better start at the beginning and explain slowly. Take your time.'

Slowly, leaving out no detail, Jane told him the story of the last few days since she had disembarked from the *Falcão*. She told the young American pilot all about her father, of her involvement in his anthropological studies, of her arrival from the *Falcão* and the finding of the indian boy in the deserted village. More emotionally she told him of the return of the *Falcão*, its wreck and the horrifying discovery of Martinez and Villas. She also swiftly recounted her version of Hugo's crash.

Hugo waited until she had finished and then gave a long low whistle.

'And you can think of absolutely no explanation for the disappearance of the villagers and your father?'

She shook her head.

'None, except that I am sure that the skeletons are those of the villagers and the European one among them is that of my father.'

Hugo broke the strained silence by holding out his cup for more coffee.

'It's a pretty tall tale to swallow, Miss Sewell.'

Jane immediately bridled.

'If you think that I am making this up . . .'

'Now hold on, lady,' Hugo interrupted sharply. 'I didn't say that at all. I was making an objective assessment. What you are saying is that there is something pretty peculiar going on around here . . . that the disappearance of the villagers and your father is also connected with the deaths of old Martinez and Captain Villas, and might even be connected with the disappearance of Lieutenant de Beja and the sudden migration of the Bakirí further south?'

Jane breathed deeply.

'I know it sounds like some sort of fantasy but what other conclusion is there?'

'But if we accept that conclusion, that's merely the start of the problem. You've then to provide the cause . . .'

Hugo looked curiously across to the young indian boy.

'You say that he doesn't speak at all?'

Jane shook her head.

'That's a pity. I guess young Chuck here could tell us a whole lot and clear up the entire spooky mystery.'

Jane gave a faint smile.

'But I don't even know for sure whether young Chuck here, as you call him, even came from this village. He answers the questions I put to him with a nod or a shake of his head but it's no guarantee that he really understands.'

'What were your plans when I . . . er . . . dropped in on you,' enquired Hugo.

'We were going to move upriver in the hope of striking a settlement or a plantation.'

'That's no good,' asserted Hugo. 'There isn't a settlement down that way for at least sixty miles.'

Jane eyed him sharply.

'Do you have an alternative?'

'Sure I do. My name, as I think I told you yesterday, is Hugo Martin. An American from Seattle in the state of Washington. I've been working in Brazil nearly two years now, flying an old Merlin for a big rancher named Xavier. He owns the biggest plantation in these parts . . . you must have heard of him?'

Jane nodded.

'I've heard people speak of him in Morená and up at Cuiaba, the capital. I think he is supposed to be one of the biggest plantation owners in the area.'

Hugo grinned.

'You better believe it, Miss Sewell. His spread is about a hundred square miles. His eastern boundary is about twenty miles from here. Well, I reckon that if we set off due east we are bound to reach his place sooner or later and we'd have a much better chance of getting there than if we headed upriver. There's some really treacherous bogs and marshes along the river and it would mean taking

48

numerous detours so the journey would be almost twice as far as you'd expect.'

'I suppose you're right,' said Jane, feeling slightly relieved at not having to make all the decisions by herself.

Hugo climbed unsteadily to his feet and stood for a moment feeling his balance.

Jane looked at him with an anxious eye.

'Don't worry,' he smiled down at her. 'Apart from feeling like death warmed up and as aching as a cowboy riding a horse with a cactus for a saddle, I guess I feel okay. Before we leave here I'd like you to show me these skeletons and I want a trip to see the *Falcão*.'

Again Jane stiffened.

'To see if I'm telling the truth?'

Hugo shook his head sorrowfully.

'You're a wee bitty touchy, lady, and I don't blame you. No, I'm not doubting your word. I just want to see if any explanations occur to me, that's all.'

Jane gazed into his eyes and immediately felt contrite.

'I'm sorry.'

It was two hours later, after Hugo had examined the village, the skeletons and the remains of the *Falcó*, that he, Jane and the boy began to pack for their journey. Hugo had lapsed into a brooding silence, a puzzled expression permanently creasing his brow as he tried to devise some plausible explanation. None was forthcoming.

Finally he shrugged and turned to helping Jane pack a couple of haversacks with tins of food from the pile in Doctor Sewell's hut.

'No need to overload ourselves,' he said. 'I'd say we'd be travelling four days at the outside, but we'll take enough for seven days to be on the safe side of things.'

Jane handed two water bottles to the boy and told him in Xingu to go and fill them from the rivulet.

Hugo gave her an admiring look.

'You speak their lingo well.'

'It's my job,' she replied shortly.

She was annoyed by Hugo's silence. She had expected him to make some comment on the mystery, to present some explanation. The thought had barely crossed her mind when she realised how irrational it was. Why should the young American be able to provide an answer to the mystery any more than she could? She realised that she was desperately hoping that some easy and acceptable explanation would present itself.

Soon they were packed and ready to move. It was midday when they emerged into the village square. Hugo held up his good hand to squint at the sun.

'We can make an easy stage today, say eight miles maybe. Then two long hauls over the following two days and we should be there.'

He grinned down at the boy.

'Okay, Chuck?'

The boy smiled in recognition of his new name.

Jane gave a final look around the village huts and tried to suppress an involuntary shiver.

It looked so normal, the huts, the forest behind them, the river . . . and yet there was that gruesome pile of bones and no living soul, except the boy, within miles. It was so inexplicable. And then there had been the horrifying end of the *Falcão* . . . the dead Martinez in the wheelhouse and the dying Captain Villas. What was the cause of it all?

'Come on, Miss Sewell,' cried the young American.

Jane made to start forward.

Abruptly she paused and cocked an attentive ear.

'Wait!' she cried.

Hugo turned and frowned.

'What is it?'

'I don't know. Listen.'

They stood for a while, heads on one side, listening.

Finally Hugo shrugged.

'I don't hear anything.'

Jane replied with an emphatic nod.

'That's just it. There is no sounds . . . and there should be sounds in the jungle. No jungle, no forest, is ever completely silent. It is as if all the animals have suddenly gone, as if there was no life here at all.'

Hugo shook his head slowly.

'Not all life has gone, Miss Sewell. Look over there, there is something alive at least.'

Jane's eyes followed his outstretched arm.

What she saw caused her to stiffen and raise a hand to her mouth. Across the further side of the clearing in which the village stood, over the white sun baked rocks, a reddy black pulsating mass was moving slowly, moving as if it was flowing across the rock. It formed a rough column.

'What . . . what is it?' she whispered.

'Nothing to be scared about,' reassured Hugo with a smile. 'It's only some ants swarming, that's all.'


## CHAPTER EIGHT

Conseulo de Silva Xavier put down her coffee cup with an angry clatter and screwed her lips into a pout of annoyance.

'But José!' she exclaimed. 'You promised that I could attend the party at the Rozinantes' place this weekend.'

Even Xavier, who had grown used to his wife's selfishness, raised his eyebrows at her callousness.

'Conseulo,' he said slowly, accenting each syllable. 'Hugo may be dead or seriously injured. He may be lying out there in the jungle alive but helpless. Yet all you can think about is the fact that we have no aeroplane to fly you to the Rozinantes' plantation to attend their party this weekend.'

Conseulo leapt to her feet, her black eyes burning in annoyance. She was very much younger than Xavier, twenty-two years old, in fact. She was small, not much above five feet, with long black hair, offset against a golden brown skin. She was extremely attractive and, if the truth were known, it was her beauty that had made Xavier into a hopeless victim of love. The only feature which spoiled her face was, in fact, her lips. They were too broad and drooped sullenly at the corners. But her figure was well shaped, though a trifle fleshy and already hinted at the full figure inclining to fat which must surely come in late middle age.

'I do not care to hear about the inefficiencies of your workers. If the Yanqui crashed, then it was his own fault. You should be able to make alternative arrangements for transportation on Saturday. I have been looking forward to the Rozinantes' party for six weeks. You know that. Why, it's the only thing in months that has broken the boring monotony of life in this God forsaken wilderness. Even the governor of the state will be there. I have bought a new dress and . . . and . . .'

Consuelo stamped her foot in temper.

Xavier looked up at her with troubled eyes and sighed.

'It is not possible to find alternative transport, Consuelo. We cannot even contact Morená at the moment. There is too much static on the radio-telephone. I think it must be the electrical storms. They are so frequent at this time of year in the sierras . . .'

Consuelo uttered a rude word which made José Joaquin de Silva Xavier wince.

'I do not want stupid excuses, José. You promised I could go to this party.'

Xavier gave a deep sigh. It was like talking to a small child, selfish, single minded. There was no reasoning with Consuelo in her present mood.

'I will see what I can do but I cannot promise.'

Consuelo turned on her heel and left Xavier to finish his breakfast alone.

Deep within himself, Xavier knew that his marriage was a mistake. He had married, or so he thought, for love. And he still believed himself to be in love with his wife. It was while he had been on a business trip to São Paulo that he had met Consuelo. When had it been? Two years ago. She had only been twenty years old. He had needed a shorthand typist to help him with his business contracts and memoranda while working in the city and had applied to an agency. They had sent Consuelo. He had been immediately attracted by her youth and her sensual, animal-like beauty. And when the young woman made it clear that she reciprocated the feelings of attraction, Xavier, nearly twenty-five years her senior, was flattered. His vanity was piqued and he fell romantically in love. And now he knew, though would not admit it openly, that she had only been attracted by the fact that he was wealthy, that he owned one of the biggest plantations in the country and could give her everything she had ever dreamed of. But within three weeks of the meeting in São Paulo, they had married. It was a simple wedding for Xavier had no relatives and the girl also had no family, or so she said.

Xavier sighed over his coffee as he remembered.

The vanity of an older man, an older and lonely man! How had he not seen through her during those weeks spent in São Paulo and Rio de Janeiro? But then, if he had seen through her, would he not have fallen for her advances all the same?

Conseulo had come from some peasant family, uprooted from their pastoral life and forced to live in the slums of São Paulo. Her selfishness, her strong self will, had been born from a desire to survive and prosper out of adverse conditions. That determination had secured her some formal education and a position as a shorthand typist . . . and, he admitted, a good shorthand typist at that. He had not seen the selfishness in her character until after they had married and returned to the Matto Grosso plantation.

From then on Xavier's life had been a constant worry. Conseulo had dominated and ruled the servants unmercifully, had created rows and problems among the domestic staff and treated the workers on the plantation as little more than serfs. Even Xavier knew that his wife, the Senhora de Silva Xavier, was called the *Senhoraca*, the would-be lady, behind her back. What was worse, she flirted disgustingly with the young men she met at parties on the surrounding plantations or when Xavier had friends to dine at his home. Their infrequent trips to Morená or Cuiaba were nightmares for Xavier. Even on the plantation itself Xavier suspected that she had flirted with Hugo Martin, though the quiet American seemed to have seen though Conseulo and conducted himself with polite remoteness towards her. No, Hugo was a good man and Xavier trusted him. But he was not sure about Juan Lopez. Although Juan had been his plantation manager for nearly four years, Xavier had never felt comfortable with him.

Xavier clicked his tongue in annoyance and buttered another roll.

What did it add up to? The fact was plain and simple. Conseulo had married him for money and position. And, realising that fact, why did he put up with her tantrums, her childish attempts to domineer him and her suspected infidelity? Was it because he loved her still? They had not even shared the same bed for the past year or so. Love needed reciprocation. Could his behaviour be attributed to the fact that in his vanity he refused to admit he had made a mistake? Or was it because his Catholicism bit deeply and would not countenance an end to the marriage? All these things Xavier had thought about many times. In the end it came down to the same explanation. José Joaquin de Silva Xavier was still infatuated by his wife.

Xavier flung down his knife in a sudden fit of temper. It was ridiculous to waste such time with negative thoughts.

'Senhor,' the lean face of Juan Lopez peered round the corner of the door.

Xavier scowled automatically.

'Excuse me for disturbing you, senhor.'

'What is it, Lopez?' snapped Xavier.

The plantation manager entered the room.

'Kanaraté has managed to get through from the western perimeter, senhor.'

Across the plantation, set at varying strategic points, Xavier had installed a system of field telephones through which workers could report in to the main plantation office when they needed help, such as extra men or supplies.

'And?'

'He says he has been searching the area there very thoroughly but there is no sign of a crash. He wants to know if he should take a jeep and press on towards Ponto Paulo.'

Xavier rose to his feet, wiping his mouth with a serviette which he then threw down on to the table.

'Of course, that is my wish. The search must be made very carefully. Tell him to go as far as the river.'

'If I may venture an opinion, senhor?'

Lopez shifted his weight from one foot to another in hesitant fashion.

'Well?'

Xavier's voice was hostile.

'If I may venture an opinion,' repeated the plantation manager, 'I would say that the search is futile. If the Yanqui crashed in the jungle . . .' Lopez paused and made a dismissing gesture with his right hand.

Xavier breathed in heavily.

'Kanaraté is to search as far as the river. Tell him.'

There was no room for disagreement in his voice.

Lopez nodded.

'Very well, senhor.'

As he went out he passed an elderly woman, a mixture of Latin and indian showing in her homely features. She bustled into the breakfast room and began to clear the table.

'You worry too much, Senhor José,' she rebuked Xavier.

'There is much to worry about, Takky,' replied the plantation owner softly.

Takky, for few could pronounce her indian name of Tacuavecé, had been working on the plantation for most of her sixty years. She had come there in the time of Xavier's grandfather and, among numerous other jobs, was the housekeeper and the cook. More than that, Xavier could treat her as a confidant, as nearly one of the family. She knew his every mood.

'Do not despair over Senhor Hugo,' nodded the old woman. 'I feel it in my bones that he is all right.'

Xavier looked at her sharply.

'How so, Takky? You haven't been consulting a witch-doctor?'

'*Deus nos!*' cried the old woman, crossing herself. 'I have been a Christian all my life, Senhor José. You know that. For what should I consult with a *pajé*? No, I pray to Our Lady that she will send Senhor Hugo back safely. I am sure she will.'

Xavier smiled wanly.

'I hope you're right, Takky.'


'Shall we push on now?'

Hugo Martin raised his eyebrows at Jane as she finished packing the remains of their breakfast into a haversack. In spite of the sleeping bags which had been salvaged from Doctor Sewell's hut, and a fire carefully built and fed from time to time by Hugo, the night had been a long and cold one. Despite the fact that it was the end of May, the hottest

55

part of the summer season, the nights were long and sometimes freezing.

Even with the late start made on the previous day, Jane, Hugo and the boy, whom they had affectionately named 'Chuck', had managed to push through the forest about seven miles or so before camping beside a small stream for the night.

Hugo reassured Jane that if the pace was kept up they would reach Xavier's plantation within two days.

Jane smiled up at the American.

'Yes, I'm ready. Where's young Chuck?'

Hugo gave a shout and within seconds the little boy appeared. He seemed relaxed and less tense than he had been during the previous two days. Jane was happy about this as she looked at him. She could not help wondering what had happened at the Trumái village and what scene had the boy witnessed there to make him so nervous and frightened.

Hugo seemed to sense the thoughts that were passing through her mind.

'We'll soon be in touch with the authorities once we get to Xavier's ranch. They'll soon clear up this mystery.'

Jane stood up and shouldered her haversack.

'Do you really think that there is a simple explanation . . . the deserted village, the skeletons, old Martinez and his boat . . .? Do you really think there is something logical about it all which can be explained?'

The pilot ran a hand through his tousled hair.

'Look, Miss Sewell, I'm just a simple airman; a flying grease-monkey, if you like . . .'

'A what?' demanded Jane.

'A mechanic . . . To me one and one add up to two. There's a logical explanation for everything in the world.'

The two adults and the boy began to push westward along a forest path.

'So how do you explain things?' persisted the girl.

Hugo raised one shoulder in a half shrug.

'I don't explain them because I don't have enough information. But that's not to say there is not a logical explanation to the situation, Jane . . . er, Miss Sewell.'

Jane gave a dismissive wave of her hand.

'Oh, for goodness' sake, let's not be so formal when we're a million miles from nowhere.'

Hugo grinned sheepishly.

'That's okay by me, Jane,' he paused and then continued, 'Now, what I was saying is this: we just have to wait until we have enough information about the problem before we can trot out glib answers.'

'But what does your instinct tell you . . . what about your imagination?' Jane said.

'I kind of guess I gave up imagination a long time ago, Jane,' drawled the pilot. 'Imagination doesn't go with combat flying . . . and, after I left the USAF I never got back into the habit.'

Jane shook her head in an exasperated fashion.

'But you must have some feeling about it? Some idea as to what could have happened.'

Hugo Martin halted and peered into Jane's eyes. He could see the apprehension in them, the need for some reassurance against the nightmare of the situation.

'I just don't have enough information,' he stubbornly repeated again. 'But if you want conjecture . . . take this move of the Bakirí tribe. You say they have lived in the same spot for hundreds of years and yet, all of a sudden, they up and move. Why? A big mystery you say. The Bakirí country lies just south of here and it's quite a remote area. What made them move out? My guess is that the crash of a SAC bomber there last month made them move out.'

Jane was puzzled.

'A sack bomber?'

'SAC,' explained Hugo. 'Uncle Sam's Strategic Air Command. Haven't you heard about it? It was the talk of Morená when I was there.'

Jane gave a negative reply.

'Well,' said Hugo, as they resumed their march, 'the United States Air Force maintain a strike force called Strategic Air Command. Twenty-four hours a day, seven days a week, they maintain long distance strike forces in the air in case of nuclear attack by certain unfriendly powers.

Most of the squadrons are equipped with B52 long-range bombers which carry nuclear payloads. Are you with me?'

'Yes,' said Jane.

'All right. Now about a month ago one of these B52s was passing over the Matto Grosso region when it went out of control and all contact with it was lost. A garbled message was picked up at Morená and it was assumed that it had crashed in the forests somewhere near Bakirí country. Search 'planes from the Brazilian Air Force scoured the area searching for it but couldn't find anything. Well, in this sort of terrain that is quite possible. You could loose several armies with all their field equipment in these forests.

'Well, the young police lieutenant, de Beja, was sent down to Bakirí country to ask the indians if they knew anything. That was when he disappeared. Now do you see what I'm driving at?'

'I think so,' said Jane hesitantly.

'We know how superstitious the Xingu indians are. Just imagine . . . one day a big silver bird crashes in on them from out of the sky . . . and a B52 is some baby, Jane. It has a wing span of 185 feet and a length of 156 feet. Imagine that floating in on you. What must they think? Wouldn't you pull up sticks and beat the hell out of there?'

Jane nodded reluctantly.

'It's a plausible explanation for the Bakirí leaving their area.'

'Too right, it is,' said Hugo fervently.

'But what about the Trumái?'

'The panic could have communicated itself to them.'

'But what of . . .'

Hugo interrupted.

'My point is,' he said, 'that when we have information we can make plausible explanations about the Bakirí and the rest . . . but, at this time, we just don't have enough information.'

Jane bit her lip.

'Okay, Hugo,' she said finally, 'You win. I promise not to mention the matter until we see the authorities.'

Privately Hugo heaved a sigh of relief. He strongly admired the determined character of this pretty English girl and did not doubt her story for one minute. Indeed, he had seen the evidence with his own eyes. But even utilising his imagination to the fullest, and he possessed imagination in quantity in spite of his denials, he could find no satisfactory explanation to assuage the girl's apprehension. Rather than add to her fears by the conjectures of his own racing mind, Hugo pretended he had no thoughts on the matter.

Jane, as she strode behind the lean, handsome American, felt a growing confusion. He was, she felt, an attractive and sensitive personality. She could read any emotions in his face as plainly as if he gave them vocal expression. Yet she could not believe him to be as unimaginative as he made out. He must have *some* ideas about the mysterious situation in which they now found themselves.

It was while she was concentrating on such thoughts that she crashed into Hugo's back.

He had come to a sudden halt, his eyes on something in the forest clearing they were just entering.

Mumbling an apology, Jane stopped and stared over his shoulder. She caught sight of something white laying in the grass ahead of them.

'Best not let the boy see this,' whispered Hugo. 'Take him round the side of the clearing.'

There was a note of command in his voice which Jane found herself obeying without question.

She and Chuck made their way along the perimeter of the clearing and waited for Hugo on the other side.

He came along a few moments later, his face white beneath his tan, and his brow creased in perplexity.

'What was it?' asked Jane.

Hugo bit his lip.

'A body?' urged Jane.

'Kind of,' admitted Hugo.

Jane suddenly realised that he was trying to protect her.

'Look, Hugo, you better tell me the truth or I'll go back there myself.'

'It was a skeleton, the bones of a man . . . a shortish man. They were picked clean just . . . just like those at the village. He had a club near one hand and some indian charm around his neck.'

Jane did not speak at once.

'Could some animal have done that?'

'Probably,' said Hugo shortly. 'Let's push on. We have quite a way to go yet.'

As Hugo took the lead again, he was extremely troubled. What puzzled him was the newness of the skeleton, the singular brightness and the lack of evidence of decomposing flesh. It was as if the skeleton had been picked clean, as if it had suddenly been dropped in a vat of acid, taken out intact and left lying on the grass.

He suppressed an involuntary shiver and, head hunched between his shoulders, pushed forward along the forest pathway with Jane and the boy bringing up the rear.

The first warning came as a coughing snarl.

Hugo jerked his eyes up to meet two tiny red inflamed jewels burning from the sleek black body of a jaguar crouched a mere twenty paces along the pathway. The ears of the great cat lay flat against its head, the head was low down on his paws and the hind legs were drawn up beneath the body in two bulks of rippling muscles.

A split second before the animal began to move, Hugo realised that the great cat was about to charge them.

# CHAPTER NINE

Even as Hugo reached towards the .38 revolver, tucked into the waistband of his trousers, he realised that it was a futile gesture. In that split second he cursed the decision to let Jane carry the rifle while he carried the hand gun which comprised their only weaponry.

The great cat had already began its charge and Hugo's hand was only halfway towards the butt of the revolver, which was a puny instrument by which to stop such a beast, when the jaguar left the ground. A split second before Hugo crashed to the ground under the terrifying weight of the beast he was aware of an explosion behind him and a scorching heat across his left cheek. Then he was down with the jaguar snarling on top of him.

Fear lent him strength, his hands clawed up to grasp the black fur around the animal's neck. Strangely, the animal's glistening jaws made no attempt to close on him and his panic-strengthened hands met with no resistance as they pushed the beast from him.

The beast rolled away, coughed hollowly and lay still.

Hugo climbed to his knees and stared at the beast. The forehead was a mass of rent flesh and blood.

'Christ!' breathed Hugo fervently.

The girl was beside him trying to help him up.

'Are you all right?' she asked anxiously, an hysterical tinge to her voice.

Hugo stood up and wiped the perspiration from his brow. He gazed wonderingly at the girl's rifle, tucked under her arm.

'Now that's what I call a fancy piece of shooting, lady,' he said softly.

Jane suddenly dropped the rifle as a fit of trembling seized her limbs. The fear and tension of the last minute suddenly struck her.

Hugo ordered her to sit down while he took out a brandy flask from one of the packs and made her swallow a mouthful of the fiery amber liquid. The boy looked on in concern.

After a moment or two Jane composed herself and gave a wan smile.

'I'm sorry . . . I never had to do that before. I was . . . was . . .' she ended lamely in a shrug.

Hugo grinned and shook his head.

'Believe me, Jane, that was the damnedest piece of shooting I've ever seen outside of Buffalo Bill's Wild West Show.'

There was admiration in his voice.

'My father taught me to shoot. He lived most of his life in the South American jungles. You need to be a good shot occasionally but I . . . I never . . .'

'You were damned fine. Saved my life.'

He left Jane wiping her face with a cold wet cloth and crossed to where Chuck was staring disdainfully down at the carcass of the beast. Examining it, Hugo saw that the animal's body had a scarred and worn appearance and, in the jaws which hung open in death, most of its teeth were decayed or broken.'

'It looks like an old cat,' he told Jane. 'I reckon that explains why it attacked us. It's too old to go after its natural prey. The deer or wild pig would be far too quick for such an old animal so it resorted to hunting nature's slowest and dumbest creature . . . man.'

Jane had fully recovered her poise.

'Did it hurt your wrist?' she asked Hugo anxiously.

Hugo glanced down at his bandaged wrist in surprised amusement.

'I forgot all about the sprain. No, I guess I'm fit. Are you okay to go on now?'

She inclined her head.

'I think you better take the rifle this time,' she said.

'Right,' he said, stooping and shouldering a haversack and the gun.

'Come on, Chuck,' called Jane and the indian boy, smiling acknowledgement of his new name, trotted obediently behind them.

Leaving the carcass of the jaguar on the path where it had fallen, the three of them set off towards their distant goal.

Conseulo de Silva Xavier reined in her bay gelding before the bungalow in which Juan Lopez lived. It was a fairly primitive white stucco building with a flat roof, typical of the adobe style, one-storey building which are popular in Mexico and many parts of Texas. It was a mile away from the main house and had originally been built for occupation by the plantation workers. Juan Lopez had asked especially if he could use the building because he felt uncomfortable living in Xavier's house under the constant eye of the plantation owner. Lopez was a solitary man who valued his privacy.

Conseulo hitched her horse to the rotting wooden rail outside the building and, taking off her broad brimmed hat, pushed into the bungalow without ceremony. She paused on the threshold while her eyes adjusted from the bright midday sunlight to the gloomy interior of the building.

There were three rooms to the bungalow. A living room

and, to one side, separated by some mosquito net curtaining, a kitchen which incorporated a small shower room, while at the back another door opened into a bedroom.

Conseulo crossed the poorly furnished and untidy living room and pushed open the bedroom door with her booted foot.

Juan Lopez lay on the bed in his trousers and vest reading a cheap paperback novel. He looked up and grinned crookedly.

Conseulo leant against the door jamb and drew in her breath.

'*Deus!* How can you live in this pigsty of a place?'

Lopez tossed the paperback aside and, leaning on one elbow, reached a hand towards an amber bottle on a bedside table. He filled a small glass to the brim and raised his eyes to the woman.

'Drink?'

She shook her head with closed eyes.

'Why don't you clean up once in a while?' she demanded.

'It suits me,' replied Lopez sullenly, swallowing his drink and immediately pouring another. He looked at her, letting his eyes travel over her trim figure, accentuated by her tight fitting blouse and riding breeches. His mouth suddenly quirked in ironic amusement. 'I make no pretensions about what I am, Conseulo de Silva Xavier.'

There was a heavy sarcasm as he emphasised her married name.

Her eyes flickered open and her breasts heaved in a surge of emotion.

'Bastard!' she hissed and suddenly launched herself across the room, her open hands, claw like, swinging towards his face.

Laughing, Lopez tossed his glass aside and his hands reached up to imprison her wrists. Using the momentum of her rush, he pulled her down on the bed, a mass of struggling, fighting wildcat. He was grinning as he pushed her over on her back and used the weight of his body to constrain her threshing limbs.

She gazed up at him with a curious mixture of hatred and desire in her eyes.

'Bastard!' she hissed again.

Lopez knelt astride her body, grinning crookedly down at her.

He said nothing but took one of his hands away from his constraining grip on her wrist. Her hand lay still. Slowly, deliberately, he placed his hand over one of her breasts, feeling its softness beneath the white cotton of her blouse and the cup of her brassiere. She lay quietly looking up at him, the black hate in her eyes glazing and dying.

'Bastard,' she whispered again, but this time there was no venom in the word, it was almost a term of endearment.

He released her other hand and slowly unbuttoned her blouse, unhooked her brassiere and began to explore the satin smoothness of her body.

A tiny moan escaped from her parted lips and she reached up with both hands and drew Lopez with a sudden violence towards her.

It was an hour later when she emerged from the shower, the water still glistening like drops of silver on her golden brown skin. She stood in the living room and began to towel herself vigorously, aware of Lopez, sprawled in his underpants in a chair, watching her appreciatively as he puffed at a cigar.

'Do you think the senhor suspects?' he suddenly asked.

Conseulo paused and sneered.

'That *estupido*? Why should he? All he thinks about is the plantation. Jesus Cristo! It is like living with a machine. He has enough money to have a house in Rio de Janeiro where we could live like decent human beings, but no! No, he shuts himself away in this godforsaken wilderness . . . for why?'

Juan Lopez shifted himself to a more comfortable position.

'To make more money, no?'

'Him? There is plenty. No, because he says that his father and his grandfather ran this plantation and so must he. That it is his duty. *Duty!*'

'Why don't you leave him if you detest him that much?'

Conseulo laughed, a short bark like laugh.

'You think I am mad? I have worked too hard to fight my

way up out of the slums to be able to live as I should live. I will not give it away now. All my life I had to fight for every crumb. Then I met José, *graças a Deus*!'

Lopez smiled.

'I find it ironic that you should thank God for José while, at the same time, you detest him so much.'

'I thank God for José's money. They say that money brings obligations, well I am prepared for that . . .' she suddenly smiled at Lopez, a voluptuous almost leering smile, and threw her towel aside. 'Yes, I am prepared to meet the obligations that go with having money, while there are other things to ease my boredom.'

She walked provocatively to the chair and stood before Lopez.

Lopez reached up and she fell willingly into his arms, her mouth hungrily fastening onto his, her tongue darting, her hands pressing.

A thunderous knocking at the door froze them where they lay.

'Senhor Lopez! Senhor Lopez! You must come quickly!'

It was the voice of old Sanchez, an elderly man who was the plantation's chief rubber collector.

Lopez bit his lip in anger.

'Get into the bedroom,' he ordered Conseulo in a whisper. 'Get your things on and wait until we are gone before you leave.'

She nodded as he called: 'One minute, Sanchez.'

He hurriedly dragged on his clothes and met the old man on the porch. Sanchez's brown leathery face was full of agitation.

'It is at the eastern perimeter, Senhor Lopez. You must come and see.'

'What is all the fuss about, Sanchez?' demanded Lopez.

'I do not know how to tell you.'

The old man spread his hands and gave a characteristic shrug.

'You must come and see, senhor,' he repeated.

Lopez sighed and motioned the old man to get into his jeep. It was a half an hour drive over a bumpy track before the eastern perimeter was reached. Along the eastern sector of Xavier's large plantation the great cotton fields were situated while nearby were a collection of shabby corrugated iron roofed huts where the seasonal cotton pickers lived during the harvest time.

Sanchez guided the plantation manager's jeep down the rough dried mud roadway, through the fields of growing plants towards the trackway which marked the perimeter of the plantation from the edge of the black, brooding jungle. There was no need for fencing around the estate. Indeed, such an exercise would have been futile against the relentless movement of the forest. Every six months or so the estate workers had to hack back the undergrowth and burn it to prevent nature reclaiming the broad strip which separated the jungle from the beginning of the cotton fields. The burnt pathway thereby acted as a deterrent to the expansion of the vegetation and as a border to the estate.

A mile or so along this pathway Sanchez signalled Lopez to stop the jeep.

'There, senhor!' he cried, pointing.

They had halted on the brow of a hillock and Lopez stood up in the jeep to see where the old man's frail hand was indicating. His mouth opened.

'Who in hell did that, Sanchez?' he said wonderingly.

Two hundred yards away it seemed as if a new pathway had been cut through the forest. There, through the middle of densely waving undergrowth of tall *sapé* grass and thickly growing bushes, was a pathway perhaps some twenty feet in width, which ran clearly through the jungle and vanished among the undulating terrain. This pathway went across the perimeter track at right angles and ran straight into the cotton fields and had eliminated perhaps a thousand square yards of cotton plants.

Lopez swore.

Some idiot seemed to be having fun with one of the harvesting machines, because the plants and the grass were levelled neatly to a faint stubble.

'Who did this?'

The old man shrugged unhappily.

'Alas, I do not know, senhor,' he said in a quavering voice. 'I was riding along the border when I discovered it.

66

As the senhor knows, I come to keep an eye on the cotton plants every other day, to make . . .'

Lopez nodded impatiently.

'Well, Senhor Lopez, I came this morning and I see this thing even as you see it now. I came straight away to tell you.'

'Someone will pay for this,' growled Lopez. 'Some fool has been having a joke, perhaps, with a harvesting machine. Thousands of dollars worth of cotton destroyed. The idiot will regret that his mother gave birth to him.'

Lopez sat back in the driving seat and sent the jeep rushing down towards the levelled area.

He climbed out and spent some time examining it before getting back into the jeep and swearing loudly.

'Only a machine can have done this. The vegetation is levelled almost to nothing. Who has been using the harvesting machines in this area?'

Sanchez hunched his shoulders again.

'I saw nothing, senhor. I heard no machine. I heard nothing.'

Lopez squinted across the levelled land.

'Well someone has done this.'

He suddenly switched on the jeep's engine and sent the vehicle careering towards the perimeter, along the newly cut pathway into the forest.

'Where are we going, senhor?' asked Sanchez apprehensively after a while.

'I want to see just how far this damned ridiculous pathway goes into the jungle and just what is at the other end of it. *Deus!* The fellow must be *louco* to drive a harvester into the jungle. He'll break it for sure.'

Lopez increased the pressure on the accelerator.

Following the strange pathway was like following a newly cut roadway, all the vegetation and many of the smaller trees had been cut down to a stubble while the larger trees remained but, strangely, shorn of all their vegetation. The pathway did not continue for long in a straight line but began to swerve in gentle curves and climb across hillocks as it followed the outlines of the terrain.

Suddenly, sweeping round the brow of a hill, Lopez and

Sanchez saw the end of the pathway and something else . . . something which sent Lopez crashing the brake to the floorboards of the jeep so that the vehicle skidded and slewed round in a complete circle, its engine stalling.

Old Sanchez half stood in the jeep, his mouth working, his watery eyes wide and horrified. With one frail hand he crossed himself.

'*Senhor Nosso!*' he whispered fervently.

Even Lopez was appalled by the reddy black pulsating mass that covered the end of the pathway to a depth of one hundred square yards and which moved slowly and irresistibly forward devouring vegetation as it went.

'What . . .' his dry mouth had difficulty forming the words. 'What in God's name is it, Sanchez?'

'Ants, senhor. They are ants.'

Sanchez shivered violently.

'I have never seen them like this, senhor. Never! But I once heard from my grandfather that such things happen.'

Even as the two men watched, large sections of green vegetation disappeared before the onward march of the broad column of pulsating blackness. Individually no more than an inch long, each ant was pressed into a large irresistible mass which seemed indestructible as it pushed forward into the forest.

'What do you mean, Sanchez?' whispered Lopez, as if afraid that the tiny insects would overhear him. 'What do you mean, such things happen?'

'They are soldier ants, *formiga-de-correicão*, senhor. Sometimes they are called legionary ants. They live by hunting and mainly eat the flesh of animals, any animals they can gain power over. They move in broad fronted columns and hunt, not as individuals but as legions, as regiments, destroying all other insect life in their path, and often the vegetation as well.'

'Incredible,' breathed Lopez as he watched the movement of the millions of insects.

'*Sim*, Senhor,' agreed Lopez. 'I have never seen them swarming in this manner though I have heard that further north some farmers have witnessed them moving in their columns and have even suffered destruction of crops from them.'

Lopez reluctantly drew his gaze away from the awesome sight.

'We better report this to Senhor Xavier,' he said. 'The other plantation owners should be warned as well.'

He started the jeep.

'Senhor!'

Sanchez' voice was almost a frightened scream.

Lopez looked up and saw to his horror that while they had been sitting in the jeep examining the ants, two columns of the insects had detached themselves from the main body and had swept in a pincer-like movement around the jeep. Even as he looked, individual insects of the vanguard of the soldier ants were climbing over the chassis of the vehicle.

Old Sanchez was hitting out at the tiny creatures with his hands as several began to swarm over him.

'Hang on, Sanchez,' cried Lopez, and sent the jeep forward.

In his nervous state he raised the clutch too quickly and the machine jumped and stalled. He switched on the ignition, the motor whirled but did not catch. More ants were beginning to climb across the jeep. Sweat began to pour from Lopez' brow. He raised a hand to dash the beads of water away from his face and felt a squelchy mess. He looked at his hand and saw several crushed insects. Fighting a desire to vomit, he became aware that his body was beginning to burn. He beat futilely at his itching flesh. Then, realising his salvation lay in getting away from the ants, he switched on the starter again. This time the engine fired.

Even as it did so there was an agonised scream from Sanchez.

Lopez turned in horror to see the old man clawing a mess of crushed insects from his eyes. Lopez could not discern which was the red mess of ants and which was blood. Sanchez was acrawl with the terrifying creatures.

The old man opened his mouth and screamed again.

Before Lopez could stop him, Sanchez had leapt from the vehicle and was running desperately through the broad reddy black column. Soon the old man's body was the same colour as the column and no longer distinguishable.

Lopez, one hand trying to brush the creatures away, sent the jeep forward.

Sanchez was on his knees screaming horribly.

The pain of a thousand bites was intolerable to Lopez. The plantation manager looked towards the fallen old man and decided that he could not help him. He must try to save himself. He bit his lip and swung at the driving wheel. The jeep skidded away from the terrible black shape which now moved feebly on the ground.

Above the racing of the jeep's engine Lopez could hear the last desperate screams of the old man.

'Senhor, senhor, for the love of God . . . *por favor, senhor, por favor* . . .'

The voice haunted him for many nights.

A mile away, Lopez braked the jeep beside a stream and without pausing raced into its swiftly flowing ice-cold current. After he had made sure that the insects were either drowned or washed away, he returned to the jeep and surveyed the reddy black mass that still clung persistently to the machine.

Lopez reached for the small fire-bottle, strapped to the back of the vehicle, and sent a jet of water washing away the creatures, pushing them from their hold.

After a few minutes, he had cleared the ants sufficiently to be able to climb back in and send the car racing back to Xavier's plantation.

He drove like one in a dream, still in a state of shocked disbelief. Once or twice he halted the jeep for he thought he heard a voice calling. It was the last agonised scream of Sanchez echoing in his mind.

'Senhor, senhor, for the love of God . . .!'

# CHAPTER TEN

Jane Sewell had never gone so deep into the jungle before. She gazed around, her eyes wide and her mind alert. A tension tightened the muscles throughout her body. The little indian boy trotted along at her side in complete unconcern. Before them, Hugo Martin strode, the rifle in the crook of his arm. He walked in a relaxed manner, now and then shifting his head left or right, towards certain jungle noises which needed identification; only the knot of muscles at the back of his neck showed Jane that he, too, was tense and alert to any danger.

Yet the forest through which they strode was strangely silent.

The forest noises which disturbed them were so infrequent as to be startling and uncanny.

It was midday on their fourth day out from the Trumái village when they came upon a clearing. It was a large rocky hill across which the myriad plants of the forest could gain no purchase for their propagation; it was a hill of gaunt granite, shot out of the earth, perhaps, in some distant volcanic dispute.

'Okay to stop here for lunch, Jane,' called Hugo over his shoulder.

'Fine. How much further do you reckon we have to go?' replied the girl, swinging her haversack from her back.

'I should guess that we'll be at the plantation by late afternoon. It's not far now.'

Chuck collected some wood for a fire while Jane unpacked some cans. While these preparations were going on Hugo scrambled up the precipitous rock face, with an agility which surprised Jane in view of the tribulations of the last few days, and stood on top of the hill looking at the surrounding forest.

'See anything?' asked Jane, laconically as he slithered down to join them over a plate of beans.

Hugo made an affirmative gesture of his head.

'Seems we are travelling parallel with a trackway. It's about a hundred yards to our left. I guess that's the one which leads up to the plantation because it's big enough to take a vehicle. Like idiots, we must have been struggling along through the undergrowth parallel to it for quite a while. It just shows you how lost you can get in this damned jungle when all the while you are just round the corner from salvation.'

Jane ladelled out more beans from the heating pan.

'So the rest of the journey should be easy now?'

'I guess so,' agreed Hugo.

'Well, I can't say I'm sorry that the experience is over.'

Hugo grinned sympathetically.

'Poor kid, it's been really tough on you these past few days . . . what with not knowing about your father and all,' he ended lamely.

Jane bit her lip. She felt cold and emotionless viewing the event in retrospect.

'I *do* know, Hugo. There is no doubt in my mind that my father is dead and that it was his skeleton I saw back at the village. The question is – who or what did it. But we've been through that before. We shall just have to wait until we see the *prefeitos* and report the matter.'

To tell the truth, the horrifying disappearance of her father and the entire village had begun to recede to the back of her mind. When she tried to formulate her thoughts on the matter, she felt puzzled. For the past four days it was the lean, soft-spoken American pilot who had dominated her thoughts until now she seemed to have known him all her life.

She knew, for instance, that he had been born and grown up in Seattle, Washington, near the Canadian border. She knew he had been keen on flying ever since he was a little boy and had, on graduating from High School and then University, where he had obtained a Bachelor of Science degree in aeronautics, joined the USAF flying fighter-interceptors.

But, he had confessed to her, that he had been unable to come to terms with military routine or the morality of warfare. He had resigned his commission and turned to civilian flying. Jobs were few and far between. He had really wanted to join a civilian airline and, unable to settle for a while, he had taken jobs as a crop-duster in Texas, Mexico and then moved further south, flying for plantation owners such as Senhor de Silva Xavier. He had worked for Xavier nearly two years now and he was thinking it was time to return home and try for a job with a civilian airline.

In fact, he told her confidentially, he had already written

off an application to a company in Seattle and he was waiting to hear from them.

He had a boyish eagerness which attracted Jane. More than that, she liked his dependability. He never became irritable or flustered. She would have panicked long ago except that his calming nature did not admit to the horrific experiences of the past few days. Hugo insisted there was a logic in everything and even the most frightening and inexplicable events derived from a logical sequence.

Jane smiled inwardly as she admitted that she was quite attracted to this tousle-haired man, with his piercing blue eyes and boyish grin.

During their walk through the jungle, Jane had reciprocated with the story of her life. Not that there was much to talk about, she mused ruefully. Her father, a social anthropologist, was always away. As she grew older, her mother used to accompany him leaving her in a boarding school in England.

The year she left school, her mother had been killed in an accident in Chile and her father returned home for a while. He had lectured at a university and providing a settled home while Jane went on to study at Manchester University. There had been no question about the subject she was to study – social anthropology. And, as soon as she had qualified, her father and herself had set off to South America to pick up his research again. She had spent a few of her schoolgirl holidays in Brazil and then several years as a student before this last trip and therefore she knew the country well and could speak both Portuguese and the Xingu indian tongue.

Hugo had been quite impressed.

One thing he detected, however, and that was Jane's heart was not really in her work. She lacked the passionate interest in her subject which was essential. She was, he felt, a prisoner of circumstances. Neither her father nor she had questioned the fact of what she must do in life. It had merely been assumed. Hugo realised that, even at this stage, Jane had not questioned that assumption. She was vaguely unhappy but did not realise the cause.

He looked across the camp fire to where Jane sat, a faraway look in her eyes as she gazed into the flames.

'A penny for them?'

Jane started.

'What?'

She turned to meet his inquisitive stare.

'A penny for your thoughts.'

A small but discernible blush crept to her cheeks.

'Oh, I was, er, just thinking that it will be nice to have a bath.'

Hugo stood up.

'Yeah, you're right.'

He waved his hands to ward off the flies which were descending on the remains of the meal.

'Well, I guess the sooner we start out the sooner we shall arrive, eh?'

'Shall we push towards the trackway?'

'Sure. The going will be a lot easier and we might meet someone from the plantation. But we should be there soon.'

'Is there a doctor nearby?'

Hugo looked at her anxiously.

'Not that I know of. Why? Anything wrong?'

'I was thinking about Chuck,' she gestured to the boy who was playing on the rocky hill. 'I've been thinking about him quite a lot . . . about his inability to talk. He can hear well, he understands when I speak to him in Xingu and he appears to know some Portuguese words. Now if he had been born mute, he would not have been able to learn Xingu or Portuguese . . . not in the primitive conditions in the Trumái village. I think his inability to speak was caused recently.'

Hugo looked interested.

'How would that happen?'

'By some sort of shock . . . I think he witnessed what happened at the village and it has made him mute. A traumatic shock, you see . . .'

Hugo shook his head slowly.

'It sounds a bit farfetched, Jane,' he said. 'Now don't get me wrong,' he raised a protesting hand as she began to open her mouth, 'I know that shocks do deprive people of the power of speech but we don't really know for sure that the kid could speak or whether, if he could speak, it has only been recently that he lost the power of speech.'

Jane sighed, shrugged and turned to clearing up the remains of the meal.

'Look, Hugo,' she turned to him suddenly, 'I agree there must be logical explanations for the various peculiar things that have been going on but, all the same, you can overdo the logical approach at times.'

Hugo looked at her for a moment and then grinned.

'Aw,' he said, kicking at the ground, 'you're probably right. But logic is the only way to keep sane at times.'

They set off through the forest again and, strangely, they became aware of a differentness of atmosphere. The sounds of the forest became many and varied. Wildlife was predominant and profuse and through the trees appeared a multitude of humming birds of many species in varying plumages of brilliant colours. There were several other species of birds, like screaming macaws in their distinctive liveries of scarlet, blue and yellow; there was the black-plumed tanagaers with the fiery red blotch on their tails. Monkeys, too, increased the noise by howling in the tree tops and the shake of the undergrowth announced the unseen presence of some larger animal.

For the first time in days, Jane began to feel more at ease with her surroundings. This was the forest she knew, not the silent brooding darkness through which they had been journeying.

After a short while, Jane, Hugo and the boy burst out into a sunlit trackway and Hugo began to lead the way at a more rapid pace.

As they came to a bend of the trackway they were abruptly halted: rooted to the spot as, just around the bend before them, there came a weird, croaking scream. It sounded once, then twice and then faded away on the hot afternoon air.

'Impossible!'

Senhor de Silva Xavier glared at his white-faced plantation manager in disbelief.

'I tell you, senhor, I saw them with my own eyes. And Sanchez . . . Sanchez is dead . . .'

Juan Lopez' voice was high pitched and there was a suspicion of hysteria edging it.

Xavier could see that the man's nerves were tautly strung. He moved to his cocktail cabinet and poured out a tumbler of whisky, watching while the man eagerly gulped it.

'But ants do not behave in this fashion, Juan,' said Xavier quietly

Lopez shrugged, a gesture of helplessness.

'I can only repeat what I saw with my own eyes.' His voice was quieter and firmer now. 'Sanchez called at my bungalow and told me of . . .'

Xavier waved a hand and cut him off in mid speech.

'Yes, yes, Lopez. You have explained this.'

He clasped his hands behind his back and walked up and down the room.

Ants do not kill human beings, he repeated to himself. Yet Lopez was not lying. He could sense that. The threat of ants was not new to Xavier, although more often than not the species of ants which damaged crops were usually confined to the extreme north of the country. The soldier ants were usually the culprits. They lived entirely by hunting and from the flesh of animals . . . any animal they could overpower but he had never heard that they would attack men. True he had known a cow, with a broken leg, eaten because it had been unable to move out of the path of a swarm of soldier ants and unable to defend itself. But *a man*! A grown, healthy man!

He moved to a bookcase and took down a volume and flicked through the pages until he came to an entry headed *Formicidae*, order of *Hymenoptra*, and a sub-heading *Eciton* species known commonly as legionary or soldier ant. He quickly confirmed his knowledge of the species. They moved in broad-fronted columns and did not hunt as individuals but as legions, destroying all other insect life. They had no fixed nesting place but bivouaced each night in a new place except when their queen was laying eggs. Each camp centred around this queen, who could lay as many as 25,000 eggs over two days. They also caused severe damage to crops.

Xavier shut the book abruptly.

Whatever the explanations, he was faced with a problem. If what Lopez said was true, and he had no reason to doubt it, a large body of soldier ants were swarming on the borders of his plantation and had already damaged his cotton fields. He must protect the plantation against further incursions. He looked across the room at Lopez.

'I must see these ants, Lopez. Drive me down there.'

Lopez set down his whisky glass unwillingly.

'I can assure you, senhor, that what I have said is the truth,' he said, a trifle sullenly.

'I have no doubt of it, Lopez,' Xavier nodded. 'But I must see what these ants are about. We cannot afford to let them spread across the entire cotton section of the plantation. We might have to burn some stretched of land to try to turn them back.'

He picked up his hat.

Lopez followed him slowly to the door.

On the verandah of the house, Conseulo was sitting sipping an afternoon drink.

She gazed up as the two men passed by with a face which mirrored bored indifference.

'More problems, José?'

She made it sound as if Xavier were always dealing with some crisis or another.

Xavier nodded absently as he walked passed her.

'Nothing to worry about, dear. Just some trouble on the cotton fields with some . . . er, insects.'

'Well, José, if that's all,' her voice rose a little, 'I want to talk to you about Saturday's party . . .'

'Sorry, Conseulo,' Xavier cut her short, 'I must go out and look at the eastern perimeter with Lopez. I'll speak you you on my return.'

The two men climbed into Lopez' jeep and sped away from the house leaving Conseulo pouting in annoyance after them.

Again, from round the bend in the trackway, came the weird, croaking scream.

Hugo raised his rifle in a defensive gesture while Jane slunk more closer to his side, the indian boy clutching tightly at her arm. For a moment or two, Hugo stood irresolute and then, to Jane's surprise, he suddenly burst out laughing.

'Hell's teeth! It's Kanaraté! Kanaraté from the plantation.'

He raised his rifle and fired two shots in rapid succession, sending all the wild life within range scattering in a profusion of noise.

Careering round the trackway came an old jeep, the horn of which was issuing forth its croaking scream. A swarthy indian was crouched over the wheel while another man clung precariously on the back of the vehicle.

The driver skidded the ancient vehicle to a halt before the group. He turned out to be an elderly man, his ancient face was wreathed in wrinkles which were now creased into a smile, showing a line of sugar blackened stubs of teeth. His black eyes twinkled at them as he leaped out and clasped Hugo's hand.

'Senhor Hugo! You are alive! *Graças a Deus!*'

His Portuguese was heavily accented and Jane automatically registered the man as a Xingu indian.

'Son of a gun, Senhor Hugo . . .' the old man's eyes swept the group and went wide as he examined Jane. '*E belo senhorinha, eh?*'

Hugo motioned him to silence.

'Jane, this is Kanaraté. Kanaraté is foreman of the indian workers on Xavier's plantation. He's been there for many years. Kanaraté, this is Senhorinha Sewell.'

Kanaraté bowed his head towards Jane.

'Sewell . . .' he mused, a frown coming to his face. 'I heard there was a Doctor Sewell living in the village of the Trumái at Ponto Paulo. Can it be that you are that doctor? Surely not, for I heard from the Trumái, who were once my people, that the doctor was an old greybeard, *não e?*'

'Doctor Sewell is . . . was the senhorinha's father,' interrupted Hugo, looking uncomfortable.

The old indian looked sharply at Hugo, a question

forming on his lips, but seeing something in the other's eye, changed the subject.

'Well, Senhor Hugo . . . you are alive. Thanks be to God. We hear that you crash, senhor. Then the Senhor de Silva Xavier sends me out to search. I take some men and search many miles through the jungle. Finally, I take the jeep with Kaluana here,' he motioned towards his silent companion, 'and set out for Ponto Paulo.'

'You've been there?' asked Hugo, a little sharply.

'No. We were on our way when I saw smoke. So we returned. It was from your camp fire, *não e*? You must have been pretty near the granite hill?'

Hugo nodded.

'We best get back to see Senhor Xavier.'

'Forgive me, Senhor Hugo! Forgive me, Senhorinha!' exclaimed Kanaraté, motioning them all into the jeep. Accompanied by Kanaraté's chatteringly, they gratefully climbed aboard the ancient vehicle which Kanaraté seemed to take a fierce pride in driving. He skidded the vehicle into a tight turn on the trackway and sent it bounding back towards the plantation borders.

'You are not hurt in your crash, Senhor Hugo?' asked the old man anxiously.

'Just shaken, I guess, Kanaraté.'

'Well,' the old man had a twinkle in his eyes, 'perhaps the Senhor will buy the new 'plane you always tell him he should buy, eh?'

'Perhaps.'

It took them under an hour to reach the perimeter fence of the plantation and perhaps a little longer to reach the main house where Takky, the plump, elderly housekeeper ran out and embraced Hugo, who was well liked by Xavier's workers. The old woman clucked like an old hen over Jane and the boy, embracing them both in broad arms whose power would have done credit to a man.

In answer to Hugo's questions, Takky told them that the Senhor was examining the eastern perimeter with Lopez while the Senhora was out riding.

Making sympathetic noises, Takky swept them all into

the house and started to run hot baths for Hugo and Jane and prepare rooms. The boy she took to her own quarters.

At times like these, Takky was in her element.

Juan Lopez braked his jeep on the brow of a hill and silently handed Xavier a pair of field glasses.

'See, senhor,' he pointed, 'down there, along that pathway . . .'

Xavier raised the glasses to his eyes and focused them for a while. For a long while he sat staring, saying nothing.

Lowering the glasses he looked at his plantation manager.

'It is as you said, Lopez. I've never seen ants massed like that before. It's incredible.'

He bit his lip and raised the glasses again. Through them he examined the mass of reddish black which seemed to look like some living organism, contracting and expanding over the ground.

'I have heard from ranchers further north about such things but I have never experienced them before. They are fairly big specimens. I do not think I can even recognise the species but they must be *formiga-de-correição* . . . soldier ants.'

'As you say, senhor,' agreed Lopez, nervously looking around the jeep. The fear of being cut off by the ants, as before, sent shivers down his spine. But the ants did not appear to be moving but were keeping to a tight circular area.

The sun was hanging low on the distant horizon.

Xavier squinted at it, one hand held before his eyes.

'I think that this must be their bivouac for the night, Lopez. Well, we must be grateful they are not on the move, eh? What I want you to do is this, send one of the boys out here to keep an eye on them tonight. Let him take one of the two-way radios to keep in touch just in case they move. But I do not think they will start to move before dawn.'

'Very well, senhor.'

'I want to know just as soon as they do start to move and I want to know exactly which way they are moving. The cotton crops must be protected and we may have to start making fire breaks tomorrow.'

He handed Lopez back the field glasses.

Lopez started the vehicle and swung it back towards the plantation.

'You can drop me off at the indian quarters, Lopez,' said Xavier after a while. 'Old Sanchez had a daughter who used to look after him. I better have a talk to her.'


## CHAPTER ELEVEN

There was no denying the tension that pervaded the atmosphere at de Silva Xavier's table that evening.

Jane shivered uncomfortably as she looked around the table.

Xavier sat at the head of the table, outwardly every bit the genial, convivial host. At the foot of the table sat Conseulo, morosely picking at her food which was served by the smiling elderly indian woman whom everyone called Takky but whose real name, so Jane learnt, was Tacuavecé. She was the Xaviers' housekeeper and had served Senhor de Silva Xavier's father before his death. On Xavier's left side sat Juan Lopez, the saturnine plantation manager, brows wrinkled in a worried frown, toying with his fork. On Xavier's right side sat Jane and beside her, Hugo.

Xavier had already done his best to dispel Jane's fears and provide some logical explanation for the events of the past few days. In fact, Jane thought, perhaps he had worked too hard at seeking an explanation which was both plausible and logical.

He had suggested that the death of old Martinez and Captain Villas had been due to an indian attack. Jane knew well that such a possibility was, theoretically, plausible. Along the Xingu many of the tribes still retained a fierce savagery and north of Morená, along the lower reaches of the vast Formosa Forest, there dwelt many uncontacted tribes who still practised the old ways such as the eating of human flesh. Certainly, it was not impossible that a tribe along the Xingu could have suddenly gone berserk and attacked Martinez' boat. However, such an explanation was entirely inconsistent with what Jane had witnessed.

Xavier had positively exuded old world Latin charm and courtesy and it was obvious to Jane that he was doing so only to allay her fears. Jane liked the courteous plantation owner but she could read his mind like a book. There was something about him which reminded her of her father.

She could see that he was very agitated himself and learnt earlier from Hugo that Xavier had drawn him to one side and confessed that he was worried that communications with Morená were dead owing to a strange static interference which rendered his radio-telephone useless. Also, it appeared that part of his cotton crops had been attacked by soldier ants and one of his workers had been killed. Now Xavier was worried by the threat of further attacks on his crops.

Jane had heard of the soldier ants who, on swarming in large numbers, devastated large areas of crops and even killed smaller species of livestock who happened to fall in their path. It was the first time, however, in her South American experience, she had heard of ants killing a full grown man.

From lowered lids, Jane examined Juan Lopez. She could see he was very drawn and haggard and his nervous playing with his knife and fork during the meal was a considerable source of irritation. Somehow, she felt, that perhaps not all Lopez' worry was attributable to the ant attack on the estate.

Next Jane considered the sulky figure of Conseulo.

She had taken an instant dislike to the sultry beauty who was introduced to her as the Senhora de Silva Xavier. She had immediately categorised Conseulo as spoilt and selfish. Jane's Portuguese was not good enough to detect the social differences of Xavier's and Conseulo's upbringing. She mistakenly thought that Conseulo was, perhaps, the product of a pampered life and over indulgent parents.

Conseulo was definitely a woman who was far happier in the company of men than women. She saw every woman as a threat to her well being and treated them in an offhand, almost rude, fashion. Jane had mentally shrugged and decided to accept the situation without protest.

During the meal, her perceptive eyes soon picked a series

of body signals between Conseulo and Lopez and there grew in her mind the realisation that the saturnine plantation manager was having an affair with his boss's wife.

Her eyes suddenly caught Xavier's and she felt the blood streaming into her cheeks. She lowered her lids, but not before she knew with grim clarity that Xavier himself had caught the direction of her gaze and in a brief second she realised that he, too, knew of the affair.

She raised her eyes again as she realised that Xavier was speaking to her.

'I beg your pardon, senhor?'

'I said, Senhorinha Jane, that you will be welcome to stop with us for as long as you like, but should you want to reach Morená to report the . . . the, er, disappearance,' he savoured the word carefully, 'yes, disappearance of your father, then Lopez here is driving to the town tomorrow.'

Lopez glanced swiftly at Xavier as if it were the first he knew of his trip.

'Thank you, senhor,' said Jane, giving a quick look at Hugo by her side as if to seek his blessing. 'I would like to stay for a while but I feel I must see the authorities in Morená as soon as possible.'

'I could drive her in,' interrupted Hugo suddenly, 'that will save Lopez a journey.'

Xavier's eyes were suddenly like gimlets as he darted a glance at Lopez. His voice was heavy.

'Lopez has to go into Morená anyway.'

Lopez tossed down his fork, clearly feeling uncomfortable.

'As you say, senhor,' he said woodenly, watching Xavier's face carefully, a hint of suspicion coming into his eyes. Did Xavier know?

At the far end of the table Conseulo smiled blithely, oblivious to the by-play.

'Good. There are several things that Lopez can fetch back for me. I want to make arrangements for the Rozinantes' party at the weekend.'

There was a silence.

'Lopez will not be coming back, Conseulo,' said Xavier heavily.

Something like a sigh escaped from Lopez' mouth. He sat still, looking before him unseeingly.

Conseulo jerked her head up, a startled look on her face.

Suddenly Lopez was on his feet.

'You will excuse me,' he muttered and turned towards the door.

'Lopez!'

Xavier's voice was like a pistol shot. As if involuntarily, Lopez halted and turned back.

'A word with you . . . in my study.'

Xavier stood up and led the way to a side door. Meekly, Lopez followed him.

Conseulo stared for a long time at the shut door, a frown on her face as if she was unable to understand the significance of the situation.

Uncomfortably, Hugo and Jane bent over the sweet that Takky was serving at the table.

Jane forced a smile at the indian woman.

'How is the little boy? How is Chuck?'

The old woman's face was a wreath of smiles.

'He is asleep now, senhorinha. There is certainly nothing wrong with his appetite for he has eaten enough to fill several full grown men. But he has uttered no word.'

'Poor little beggar,' muttered Hugo. 'Can't he be naturally mute?'

Jane shook her head.

'I'm almost sure, Hugo. He can understand speech and, as I said before, if he were naturally mute, how would he have learnt to understand speech in a primitive village?'

There was a sudden crash of cutlery which coincided with the study door being opened and Lopez emerging red faced. Conseulo stood up, dropping her knife and fork. For a moment Lopez' eyes met hers and then dropped. He turned hastily on his heel and went out.

Ignoring the presence of Jane and Hugo, Conseulo crossed the room to the study door, her face working and she was almost screaming at Xavier before she reached the door.

'What is the meaning of this scene?' she was demanding in strident tones. 'What have you been saying to Lopez . . .?'

The door slammed shut behind her.

Her voice continued on a high note.

The old woman, Takky, still smiling was cleaning away the plates as if nothing unusual were taking place. She caught sight of Jane's startled glance and shook her head.

'Do not worry, senhorinha,' the old woman made a half shrug of one shoulder, 'such things frequently happen, is it not so, Senhor Hugo?'

She appealed to the American for support.

Without waiting for an answer she leaned close to Jane and dropped her voice to a whisper: 'Ah, the young senhora is not good for the master. She does not belong in our country. But how can you tell a man who thinks he is in love?'

Clicking her tongue, the old woman bustled out of the door.

Xavier's voice could suddenly be heard drowning the high pitch tone of her voice. It was not a pretty sound. *'Indecente . . . sordida . . . de moral baixa . . .'* and other descriptions of the uncomplimentary view of his wife echoed through the door.

Abruptly the voices cut off to a hysterical crying and a door slammed on the far side of the room.

After ten minutes Xavier re-entered the room. He looked calm and immaculate.

Without a word he resumed his place at the head of the table.

There was a minute or so of uncomfortable silence and then he smiled softly at the couple.

'Will you join me in a brandy or some other liqueur?'

His troubled eyes met those of Jane and Hugo.

'You . . . you will forgive our slight domestic problem, Senhorinha Jane,' he said slowly. 'Hugo knows that Conseulo, Senhora de Silva Xavier, tends to be somewhat flirtatious, capricious, *não e*? It is on account of her age. Sometimes, like a young untrained filly who tries to kick over the traces, she must be taught that it is a wrong thing that she does. The source of her flirtations must be removed.'

He paused.

'About that brandy now?' he introduced an unnaturally bright tone into his voice.

Hugo and Jane nodded slightly and watched Xavier pour forth the drinks from a cut glass decanter. He handed them the drinks and then produced a box of cigars.

'Hugo does not smoke, I know, but you will forgive me, senhorinha, if I indulge? I know it is a disgusting habit but I am too long in the tooth to change a habit of a lifetime, even though I frighten myself every time I read those learned medical treatise on the evils of smoking.'

'Go ahead,' smiled Jane. 'Don't mind me.'

'You are too kind, senhorinha,' acknowledged Xavier with a bow of his head.

There was a silence while he lit his cigar.

'I have sacked Lopez,' Xavier suddenly said. He paused and looked at Hugo. 'I have sacked Lopez,' he repeated, 'and he will leave tomorrow. He will drive into Morená and take Senhorinha Jane to the *prefeitos*. If the senhorinha will then, perhaps, deliver some letters for me? I must inform the authorities of the attack on my cotton crop and the death of poor Sanchez. I must also try to establish some communication with Morená.'

'I'm surprised that you are getting a continuous electrical static on the radio-telephone,' observed Hugo after Jane had agreed to deliver Xavier's letters for him.

Xavier waved his cigar towards his study.

'Come, let me demonstrate.'

They followed him into the study and he went to the radio-telephone, switched on and fiddled for a while with the dials. Then he handed Hugo the ear-phones.

Hugo listened to the crackling and started to twiddle the various knobs and dials, a frown creasing his brow.

'It certainly is an electrical interference. I can't say that I've ever encountered it before.'

Xavier switched off the machine and shrugged.

'It's been like this for several days now. I think it must be something to do with the electrical storms we have at this time of year. Anyway, there is just no way to get in touch with Morená, except by the road. It is a two day journey, senhorinha, either by road or by river. Both routes take about the same time.'

Jane nodded.

'Very well, senhor.'

Hugo gave a sudden chuckle.

'Well, senhor, you cannot deny that I was right about the old Merlin, eh? You certainly needed a new aircraft.'

Xavier gave a grin which seemed out of character with his old dignity.

'Yes, Hugo, You were right. It is a pity that you had to demonstrate the fact in the hard way, *não e?*'

'A good thing for me, though, senhor,' smiled Jane. 'If I had not had Hugo with me, I doubt whether I should have survived the jungle.'

'Oh?' replied Hugo, 'And who was it that pulled me out of the 'plane and patched me up?'

For a few seconds their eyes met and held until Xavier broke the embarrassed silence.

'Well, it is a good thing for both of you, eh? Come, let us have another brandy, then I suggest we turn in early.'

Later that evening Hugo and Jane sat out on the verandah looking at the blue-black canopy of the heavens, studded with a myriad of twinkling white pin pricks. The cold chill of night had not yet swept across the forests and the evening was still warm and smelt of the fragrance of many flowers.

'I'd like to see you again, Jane,' said Hugo softly.

Jane gave him a quick smile. She found her heart beating a little faster as she looked on this tall, fair-haired American who, at one and the same time, could be both so masculine and yet so shy and boyish.

'I'd like that, too,' she replied.

'It's a pity Xavier had to sack Lopez. I could have driven you to Morená. In fact, I'm thinking of quitting Xavier. After all, I've been down here a couple of years now and saved up a little.'

Jane gave him a searching look.

'What would you do? Continue trying to join an airline company?' Hugo nodded, smiled and drew from his pocket a letter.

'Remember I told you that I had applied for a job with an airline in Seattle?'

Jane nodded.

'Their reply was waiting for me today. It had been here for the past week. I'm accepted on condition that I pass all their medical tests. They give me two months to report to them in Seattle.'

The girl laid a hand on his arm.

'Hugo, I'm so pleased for you.'

Hugo smiled happily.

'Guess it's what I've always wanted . . . being an airline pilot, that is, and being based back in my home town in Seattle.'

Suddenly his face was serious again.

'But I guess I can't leave the old man, Xavier, with all this trouble at the moment. With Lopez gone, I'll have to give him a hand out, that is until he gets another estate manager.'

There was a silence.

'You are not going to hurry off anywhere, are you Jane?'

The girl was puzzled.

'How do you mean?'

'Like back to England.'

She shook her head.

'Not for a while. When I get to Morená, I shall probably have to stay there a while until the *prefeitos* can make a report on the disappearance of my father, not to mention the strange deaths of Martinez and Villas.'

Hugo's eyes suddenly brightened.

'If you have to stay in the area, why not drive back here and stay at the plantation? Kanaraté can go in with you and Lopez and then drive you back.'

Jane looked dubious.

'What about Senhor Xavier . . .?'

Hugo snorted.

'Sure he'll say it's okay. We'll ask him first thing in the morning. How about it?'

Jane let her feeble resistance be overcome.

Hugo's happiness was infectious.

'All right.'

Suddenly a shadow was thrown across the verandah.

Hugo looked up startled.

It was the lank figure of Lopez.

'Pardon,' he said gruffly. He was carrying two old battered suitcases. 'Your pardon that I startled you.'

Hugo gazed at his suitcases.

Lopez followed his gaze.

'I've packed ready for tomorrow. I shall stay in a spare room here tonight rather than in my shack. It will save time in the morning. You can have the old adobe house if you want it now.'

Hugo shook his head.

'I'm sorry things had to end this way for you, Lopez,' he said, awkwardly.

He had never entirely liked Lopez but somehow he felt sorry for the man. If anyone was to blame for the situation, he felt it was Conseulo rather than Lopez.

Lopez lifted one shoulder and let it fall in a gesture of resignation.

'Senhor Xavier is quite justified,' he said, surprising both Hugo and Jane.

'What will you do?' asked Hugo.

Lopez spread his hands.

'Oh . . . there are several jobs open for a good plantation manager. I am not worried.'

'Do you have enough cash to get by on?'

Lopez laughed hollowly at Hugo's question.

'Oh yes. Senhor Xavier made sure of that. Well, goodnight senhorinha . . . goodnight, Martin.' He turned on his heel and was gone into the house.

Hugo sat looking after him for a moment and then bit his lip and sighed.

'I feel sorry for him,' he explained in answer to Jane's query. 'That's why I was going to offer him some cash.'

'You think Conseulo is really the leading spirit in that affair?'

Hugo nodded his head emphatically.

'She's really a nasty little piece of work, Jane.'

Jane assented by her silence.

Hugo stood up and stretched his legs.

'Time to hit the sack, I guess.'

He helped Jane to her feet. They stood looking at each other a moment.

89

'Goodnight, Jane.'

He shuffled his feet for a second and then stuck out a hand.

Suppressing a smile, Jane solemnly took it. They stood holding hands for several seconds before, with an embarrassed cough, Hugo let go and turned into the house with a hoarse 'Goodnight'.

Jane stood gazing after him, a frown furrowing her brow. Then she turned towards her bedroom, her face wreathed in smiles.

## CHAPTER TWELVE

Jane came awake suddenly and lay for a moment wondering what had caused her to start from her deep sleep.

It was still dark. She could hear the weird nocturnal sounds of the forest coming through her half opened window in spite of the shrouding thickness of the mosquito net that was draped over her bed. With a sigh, she turned on her side and glanced at the luminous dial of the gently ticking clock. It was nearly three o'clock.

She was about to close her eyes again when the sound came.

Her forehead compressed in a frown.

It was a strange sound; it came firstly like the distant murmur of the sea, pulsating with a slowness of rhythm which was quite hypnotic. As she lay there listening, a great feeling of drowsiness came over her. Her eyes blinked once or twice in an effort to remain open and then drooped in a half closed state. Her breathing came deeply as if she was asleep.

A tiny conscious part of her brain began to clamour a warning but no sooner had the thought flashed in her mind that she was being hypnotised than the thought faded and was gone.

The noise grew in volume, still louder and then ebbing like the distant sea.

Then through the whispering murmur came a higher

pitched tinkling. It seemed to Jane as if, in the tinkling, there came the sound of voices. Voices, and yet the voices conveyed no words; no words but there was a tremendous urgency about the voices. It was almost as if they consisted of millions of tiny tinkling crystals being blown by a gentle wind.

Slowly Jane sat up.

Again a panicked thought flashed through her mind to be engulfed by the soft reassurance of the murmuring sea.

She was standing before her window like some somnambule; then moving hesitantly in a sleeping walk to open the shutters and stare with unseeing eyes out into the blackness of the night.

A hundred yards away from the house stood a small patch of forest. Xavier had never destroyed it because he wanted a cluster of trees near the house. He had often expressed his belief that trees, giving off oxygen, were vital to man's existence and therefore made the quality of man's life better by purifying the air, especially in the vicinity of man's home. But now it was from this forest that the noises, the soft murmuring sea, were emanating. And, perhaps it was merely the moonlight dancing on the flickering leaves as they moved in the gentle night breeze, but it looked as though dozens of pin pricks of white light were moving amongst the trees.

For several moments Jane stood at the window, heedless of the breeze flapping at her thin cotton nightdress.

Slowly, unwillingly, her lips tried to form words.

'I . . . I am here.'

The tinkling voices rose and ebbed again.

There was a deep urgency in the tinkling.

A faint thrill of resistance, sparked by that tiny conscious part of her mind, ran through Jane. She seemed to hesitate. Then the tinkling crystal sounds rose and fell, fell and rose, urging and pressing.

Jane climbed over the window sill out onto the verandah and, without haste, began to walk along its wooden floor to the railings. Heedless of their impediment, she swung her long legs over them and dropped the few feet to the darkness of the lawn which surrounded the main house.

With regulated strides, still walking as if in her sleep, Jane moved towards the blackness of the forest with its tiny dancing white lights. As she drew nearer, the murmuring voices began to raise to a crescendo, encouraging, enticing, imploring her to hasten. A gale seemed to be blowing through the hanging crystal, so violent was its tinkling.

Jane felt the urge to run into the forest, some magnetic force was pulling her towards it, but somewhere, somewhere deep within her, that spark of resistance refused to be crushed and caused her to brake her uncontrollable limbs.

She had reached the edge of the forest now.

It was as if she was standing in a room full of long crystal chandeliers which were being rocked by a strong breeze.

The noise seemed all around her. She held out her arms as if to say 'I am here'. The noise seemed to converge, to begin to swallow her . . .

A single, shrill scream cut through the noise.

Then there was total silence.

At once Jane started from her somnambulistic state, eyes wide with terror.

The forest lay in black, forbidding silence. Even the chirping of the crickets no longer existed. The great trees lay before her, rising from their covering of undergrowth, tall, black fiends from hell. There were no lights, no murmuring, no tinkling crystal.

She felt her body shaking in the cold night air and realised that the sweat was pouring from her.

There was a momentary sickness; she swayed and caught her balance by leaning one hand against the trunk of a tree. She inclined her head forward and inhaled deeply several times in an effort to clear her head.

Lights had flashed on in the house behind her. Voices were raised in query and the lights on the patio were suddenly flooded on.

Xavier and Hugo, clad only in pyjamas, were racing across the lawn towards her while other figures congregated on the verandah.

Hugo was the first to reach her and sweep his arms around her.

'Are you all right, Jane? What in hell's happened?'

She could not reply but lay for a moment shivering in the security of his arms.

'Jane, darling?'

Her bewilderment and fear began to fade and a small smile of contentment caught at her mouth.

Hugo peered down anxiously at her tight shut eyes.

Even in the darkness Jane could sense the apprehension in his body.

'I'm okay, Hugo. It's, it's all right.'

Xavier hovered anxiously holding a torch.

'Why did you scream, Senhorinha Jane?' he asked.

Jane drew herself up and peered round in puzzlement.

'I didn't. It was the scream that woke me.'

'Woke you?' Xavier frowned. 'You mean, Senhorinha Jane, you were sleepwalking?'

Jane shrugged her shoulders.

'I . . . I must have been, otherwise, how did I get here?'

'We must go back to the house,' interrupted Hugo. 'She'll catch her death of cold like this.'

Xavier agreed.

'But if it was not the senhorinha who screamed, who was it?' he added.

He swept his torch in an arc.

A small figure moved in the darkness.

'Who is it?' Xavier demanded.

Jane was the first to move.

'Why . . . it's Chuck!'

The small boy looked at her with tear-stained face and then threw himself into her arms sobbing. But between the sobs there were forced out words in the Xingu language . . . words!

Jane held him by the shoulders and looked at him in amazement.

'Chuck! Chuck, you can speak! Hugo, he can speak!'

Xavier ushered them to the house and into his study where he opened a brandy bottle. Takky, awake and clucking like a mother hen, bustled off to their rooms to bring their dressing gowns.

Lopez stood in a corner looking on with wide eyed bewilderment while Conseulo, sulky and pouting at being disturbed, draped herself in one comfortable chair by the remains of the previous evening's fire. Xavier bent and rekindled the ashes into a blaze while Hugo attentively hovered over Jane and the small boy who continued to sob out his story to the girl.

'Well, Senhorinha Jane,' said Xavier, standing up as the flames begun to roar up the chimney from the wooden logs. 'We'd better hear what happened.'

Jane briefly recounted her experience to Xavier who gave her all his attention, a serious expression on his face. Conseulo sat with a sneer of disbelief on her face while Lopez was wide-eyed in horror. Hugo was the only one who never questioned her veracity.

Xavier stood before the fire, hands behind his back, his face puckered into a frown.

'Let me clarify the situation, Senhorinha Jane,' he said slowly. 'You say you were awakened by a noise, "tinkling voices" you described it as. These "voices" enticed you to go to the forest. Is it not so?'

Jane agreed, realising how stupid the whole thing sounded.

Hugo gave her arm an encouraging squeeze.

She smiled her gratitude for his support.

'It is an odd story, Senhorinha Jane,' said Xavier. 'And now, you say, this Xingu boy who you found mute and wandering in the forest, screamed and broke the hypnotic trance which you were placed under. And now he had found his tongue again.'

Conseulo gave a giggle which died after Xavier turned on her with a withering look.

Xavier turned back to Jane with a gentle sigh.

'Senhorinha, I must ask you this, are you given to sleepwalking?'

Jane bit her lip.

'I know how fantastic it sounds, senhor, but I swear what I tell you is the truth. I have never been given to sleepwalking in my life.'

'I believe her,' said Hugo emphatically.

Xavier looked at him with a gentle smile.

'You will forgive me, Senhor Hugo, if I point out that you are perhaps a little partisan in this affair, *não e*? But I would incline to agree that if the senhorinha was in reality sleepwalking then the trauma of being awakened from a somnambulistic state would have left a marked effect. But we must question the boy. Perhaps, Senhorinha Jane, you will translate . . .?'

'I can speak Portuguese, senhor.'

The company turned and looked towards the boy in surprise.

'My name is Uuatsim of the Trumái and I received learning from the missionaries of Cristo.'

The frightened little boy now held himself up with a strange dignity, meeting the gaze of the assembled people firmly without waving.

Xavier smiled gently at him.

'Well, tell us, Uuatsim of the Trumái, was it you that screamed?'

The boy nodded solemnly.

'Tell us what happened, Uuatsim.'

'I was asleep on the verandah, senhor . . .'

'On the verandah?' interrupted Xavier. 'Were you not given a bed in the quarters of my housekeeper?'

'I am of the Trumái, senhor,' replied the little boy with the gravity of an old man. 'We are a tribe of hunters who dwell in the great forests. We have no use for the stifling bags which you call beds. It is better to sleep on the warm, living bed of the mother who gives us all things.'

Xavier smiled but kept his tone solemn.

'Indeed, Uuatsim of the Trumái. And so you were sleeping on the verandah . . .?'

'I was, senhor, and was awoken by the Senhorinha Jane climbing through her window . . . and at once I became awake of the sounds, sounds which I have heard once before . . . sounds such as you hear when you stand in front of the entrance to a great cavern while the wind is whispering across it. I saw the senhorinha go towards the noises, she moved like one who is asleep and I knew she did not go willingly.'

The boy paused.

'Go on,' urged Xavier.

Conseulo yawned.

95

'This is all so ridiculous,' she muttered. Her husband turned and gave her a hard stare and she relapsed into a sulky silence.

'Go on, Uuatsim,' urged Jane softly.

'I feared for the senhorinha, who had been my good friend. I wanted to cry out and warn her. But for these past few days the spirits of my ancestors have wrested the speech from me. I strained and I strained in order that speech might come back to me.'

The boy's voice faltered.

'Then the gods of my ancestors be praised! My voice was found again and I screamed and awoke the senhorinha.'

Xavier stroked the side of his nose with a forefinger.

'Tell me, Uuatsim, when did you lose your voice?'

It was the first time I heard the evil noise, senhor. It was just before the coming of the ants.'

'What?' Xavier's voice snapped like a steel spring.

'Before the coming of the ants, senhor. Many days back the ants came to our village . . .'

'Which was your village, Chuck, er, I mean Uuatsim?' demanded Jane quickly.

The boy turned to her with a smile.

'It is all right, Senhorinha Jane. You and the Senhor Hugo may continue to call me Chuck. It is our special name is it not?'

Jane nodded with a fleeting smile.

'But which was your village, Chuck?'

'Why, senhorinha, the one at which you found me . . . the place the missionaries of Cristo call the Ponto Paulo.'

Jane let out her breath sharply.

'Then you knew my father, the doctor?'

The boy nodded gravely.

'But they are all gone now, the doctor and my people. The ants have taken them.'

Conseulo gave a hysterical laugh.

'What is all this nonsense, José? It is upsetting me. And I am losing my beauty sleep. What is the child rambling about?'

'Conseulo, please be silent,' snapped Xavier. 'If you cannot remain quiet, please go back to bed.'

Conseulo sprang up as if she had been slapped.

'Very well! I shall leave you to your ridiculous, childish games!'

The study door crashed shut behind her.

There was silence for a moment before Xavier turned back to the small boy who was the focus of their attention.

'Now, Uuatsim,' coaxed Xavier, 'perhaps you had better begin at the beginning. Tell us about the ants.'

'I'm hungry,' the boy suddenly announced.

Xavier gestured at Lopez.

'Get something for him to eat from the kitchen.'

For a moment Lopez looked as if he were about to refuse but he turned and sullenly left the room, returning shortly with some bread and cheese. Chuck began to munch it eagerly.

'Come on, Chuck,' urged Hugo. 'Don't hold out on us.'

'I will tell you, Senhor Hugo, but I do not remember a great deal.'

The small boy paused and puckered his brow as if trying to dredge up the memories.

'It seemed to start when hunters from the country in which the sun goes to sleep came to our village. They told us that a big silver bird, in whose body strange men flew, or so they said, had fallen into the forests with a great noise and fire.'

'That must have been the B52 crash, the one which the authorities never found,' said Hugo, looking across to Xavier.

'Tell me, Uuatsim,' said Xavier, 'did these hunters come from the land of the Bakirí.'

The boy nodded, his mouth full of bread.

'Yes, senhor. They were Bakirí hunters. My father told me never to go near them for they are dirty people and not to be trusted.'

'And they told you that the great silver bird had crashed in their country?'

'I have said so, senhor,' affirmed the boy.

'Go on, Uuatsim,' urged Jane.

'It was said that the noise and fire of the silver bird had woken the great Igaranhá . . .'

'The what?' queried Hugo.

This time it was Jane who answered.

'It is a malevolent spirit which is greatly feared by the Xingu. It is said that it demands blood sacrifice to propitiate it.'

'I see,' said Hugo in a voice which indicated he did not think much about the idea of rampaging gods.

'Many of our finest warriors and hunters were sent forth,' continued the boy, 'they were told to seek out the great god and make sacrifice. But they never returned.'

The boy paused and shuddered slightly.

'And?' prompted Jane.

'Then one day I was sent to tend to the sheep flocks of the village. We kept the sheep tether on a hill above our village. The senhorinha will know of it . . . it is a rocky hill on which there are many caves.'

'I know it,' affirmed Jane.

'It was about the hour of the high sun. I was on the hill when I heard a strange sound, that murmuring of the wind which I heard again tonight. At first I did not know what it was. It was like the wind when it whispers across the mouth of a great cavern.

'I did not know what to make of it, I looked about me but could see nothing. And then I looked down the hill towards the village. At first I could see nothing unusual. Then I noticed my people were all standing still as if in attitudes of listening. Then, after a little, the doctor, the old senhor, your father, Senhorinha Jane, came from his tent walking like one in a trance. It was the same walk, the same trance, as you had tonight, Senhorinha Jane. He walked into the jungle. I did not see him again.'

There was a long silence.

'And then?' urged Xavier. 'What happened then?'

'And then,' the boy shuddered violently, 'then the ants came . . .'

# CHAPTER THIRTEEN

There was a long silence before Xavier cleared his throat and spoke.

'How,' he demanded, a sudden urgency edging his voice, 'how did they come.'

'They swarmed like soldier-ants, senhor,' replied the boy. 'They were larger and stronger than those I have seen in the forests but they swarmed into the village destroying . . . I . . . I saw several people covered by them until, after a while, only their bones were left. I . . . I do not remember much else except that I stood on the hill and screamed until a blackness came over me and I awoke in the evening. I went down to the village but there was no one there. I tried to shout for help but I found that the gods had taken my tongue from me and I could not speak. Later, I do not recall how much later, the Senhorinha Jane found me.'

Suddenly, his recital at an end, the dignified little indian collapsed into the small frame of a sobbing child.

Jane took him in her arms and tried to comfort him.

Hugo glanced at Xavier and raised his eyebrows.

The plantation owner imperceptibly inclined his head towards a corner of the room and the two men moved themselves into it. Lopez curiously followed them.

'What do you make of that, boss?' whispered Hugo.

'A strange tale.'

'But not an impossible tale!' hissed Lopez.

Xavier gave him an unfriendly glance.

'We must leave doubt for a child's imagination. Nevertheless, I am inclined to believe there is a considerable element of truth in it.'

'But ants don't attack people,' protested Hugo.

Lopez gave a sardonic bark of a laugh.

'You would not say that if you had seen what I saw this morning. If you had seen the ants swarming over poor Sanchez . . .'

'An old man is one thing,' said Hugo. 'I have heard that

99

soldier ants have eaten an entire cow who lay sick in their path . . . but the child is asking us to believe that a swarm of ants surrounded a large indian village and ate all the people. That's ridiculous.'

Xavier shrugged.

'You have an alternative explanation, Hugo?'

'No,' admitted the American. 'But I cannot accept this idea. It's too much like science fiction.'

'No, Martin!' Lopez' voice was harsh. 'It is very simple. The soldier ants are not just attacking crops, they are attacking people!'

Jane's head jerked up at the stridence of Lopez' voice and she stared at them over the head of the little boy.

'I better take Chuck to my room. He's almost asleep already and he needs some rest.'

'So do you, Jane,' agreed Hugo. 'I'll look in before I turn in to see if you are okay.'

She smiled, a short, nervous smile, which embraced the company and left with the sleepy-eyed boy.

As the door closed Hugo turned back to Xavier.

'Come on, senhor,' he exhorted, 'surely you don't believe in this idea of man-eating ants?'

'Have I not said that I have seen them, Martin?' demanded Lopez. 'I saw poor Sanchez . . .'

He was stilled by Xavier's upraised hand.

'Hugo, my friend, flesh-hunting ants are not so incredible as you may think. We have such a species in Brazil, as you know. The soldier ants live entirely by hunting and from the flesh of any animals they can overpower. They do not hunt as individuals but as legions and move about in broad-fronted columns. Now man is a difficult animal to overcome but that does not mean to say that he would be an impossible victim for a swarm of these soldier ants. It is true that they have been known to eat a whole cow because it lay in their path. Whole crops and plantations have been devastated by such ants. When they swarm across the land they will eat any animal who falls in their way. It is not so incredible, merely unusual.'

Hugo shook his head in disbelief.

'But attacking a helpless animal is one thing, senhor. To

attack a full grown man, let alone devastate an entire village of people, is beyond comprehension. It is too fantastic even to contemplate.'

'Pah!' spat Lopez, 'had you seen what I saw this afternoon . . . Well, I am glad I am leaving in the morning because I am sick of this godforsaken country.'

He turned and slammed from the room.

Xavier took out a cheroot from a silver case and carefully lit it.

Hugo waited for him to make some comment but the plantation owner said nothing.

'What should we do?' ventured Hugo after a silence which became slightly embarrassing.

'Do?' Xavier jerked himself from his reverie. 'I think we must leave this affair until tomorrow. I have a man posted to keep watch on the ants' nest near the eastern perimeter. I suppose bivouac is the correct name for it. If they make a move towards the plantation then I shall have to burn an area of land in order to turn them back from the cotton fields. They have already written off a considerable amount of the crop. But we shall get plenty of warning this time.'

'And you really believe young Chuck's explanation?' persisted Hugo.

'I believe that the ants seem to be constituting a threat, at the moment,' said Xavier vaguely.

'And the noise? Jane's sleep walking?'

Xavier hesitated. He had almost forgotten the reason why they had been awoken from their sleep.

'Frankly I do not know. It is only the boy who links the two things together by saying he heard the same noise tonight that he had heard before his village was attacked by ants. He and Jane were the only ones who heard that noise, by the way.'

Hugo looked at Xavier sharply.

'Do you mean to imply . . .?'

'I imply nothing. I state the facts.'

Hugo was suddenly struck by a thought.

'Senhor, it occurs to me . . . what we have heard so far about the behaviour of the ants is in keeping with the behaviour of the soldier ant species?'

'That is so, except in one important aspect.'

'Exactly,' Hugo cut him short. 'That aspect being that it is unusual for them to attack men, much less destroy a village.'

Xavier nodded.

'What is your point, Hugo?'

'The point is that the boy said the trouble started when the B52 crashed in the jungle. Jane also said that Captain Villas told her that he was going into Bakirí country because they were leaving the area; the same area where Lieutenant de Beja disappeared.'

'So?' said Xavier softly. 'The mysterious behaviour of the ants commenced after the crash of the American bomber? Is that the point?'

'Yes,' said Hugo, earnestly. 'Is there not a possibility that the two things are linked? The B52 was a Strategic Air Command bomber. She carried a crew of six and a nuclear payload. We know that she went down south in Bakirí country but even the Brazilian Air Force couldn't locate the crash. Soon after this, the Bakirí started to move out of the area. Then we get a number of deaths, reportedly from attacks by ants swarming from the direction of the Bakirí country.'

'Do you have a conclusion, Hugo?' asked Xavier quietly.

'Do you think that these particular swarms of ants could have been effected by leaking radiation from the missing B52's weaponry?'

Xavier looked at his pilot long and thoughtfully.

'You mean that these ants could be some form of mutant of ordinary soldier ants who happened to be nesting near the spot where the B52 went down? That the mutant aspect in them causes them to attack men which they would not normally do unless the man was lying in their path and unable to defend himself?'

'Something like that,' agreed Hugo.

Xavier stood up, stubbed out his cheroot and stretched himself.

'I give you a certain logic there, Hugo. But I think the hour is late and we might be given to fantasising a little. I think we should best sleep on the matter, *não e*?'

Hugo's mind was spinning with a million thoughts as he made his way along the corridor of the house towards Jane's room.

The door to the spare room which Lopez was occupying suddenly swung open and Conseulo came out and had shut the door before she realised that Hugo was approaching. She started and then drew her flimsy black silk gown round her. Hugo could see that she was not wearing anything underneath. She drew herself up and her red lips twisted into a cynical sneer before she pushed past Hugo and made towards her own bedroom. Hugo said nothing but stood aside to allow her to sweep by. He was sad for Xavier but it was none of his business to interfere.

He paused a moment outside Jane's door and listened.

It was quiet and he wondered if she were asleep. He tapped gently on the wooden panels and almost at once her voice answered: 'Hugo? Is that you?'

He entered quietly, closing the door behind him.

The room was in semi-gloom. The windows were firmly shut and a fire had been rekindled in the fireplace against the bitterly cold nights which the dry season produces. On a chaise longue, which stood against one wall, Chuck lay cocooned in a blanket, his deep breathing proclaiming him to be asleep. Jane was lying in bed but, as he entered, she pushed herself into a sitting position.

Hugo moved forward and perched himself on the edge of the bed.

'You okay, love?' he whispered. 'I thought you'd be asleep by now, like young Chuck.'

He waved towards the sleeping boy.

She smiled.

'I was waiting for you. I wanted to know what you and Xavier thought about the story Chuck told . . . about the ants.'

Hugo ran through a resumé of the conversation.

Jane listened in wide-eyed horror.

'But could ants, even a mutant form, really devour a whole village . . . my father, Villas, Martinez . . .?'

She suppressed a shudder and Hugo lent forward and took one of her hands in both of his.

'It's possible, I guess, Jane. And what it boils down to is this, Xavier and I will have to destroy this swarm. I think Xavier is writing a report of the matter now for you to take into Morená tomorrow.'

'It seems a bit fantastic, doesn't it?' Jane whispered, 'Mutants killing people. And then there was those awful tinkling voices. I can't understand it, Hugo.'

This time she was unsuccessful in suppressing the shiver that ran down her back.

Hugo bent forward and placed an arm around her shoulders. She lay for a moment passively and then raised her head to his, her lips were slightly parted and she lay still, her attitude clearly an invitation, her eyes half closed as Hugo bent forward to kiss her.

To Hugo it was like the experience of drinking an ice cold glass of water after a walk in the desert. It was the experience of a pleasant, tingling shock.

It was he who finally broke the embrace and started up red faced and slightly embarrassed.

'Guess we . . . guess we better talk in the morning,' he said, awkwardly.

Jane felt a wave of tenderness at his gauche shyness. It brought forth some maternal streak. She raised a hand to his cheek and stroked it softly. Then, abruptly, she placed her hand on his neck and fiercely drew his head down to hers again. When they drew breath again, she shifted in the bed and demurely drew back the sheets.

'Stay with me, Hugo,' she said softly.

There was no gauche shyness as he took off his dressing gown and climbed in alongside her warm, inviting body.


## CHAPTER FOURTEEN

Hugo awoke to find Jane bending over him and shaking him. He blinked his eyes, his mind sluggish and still half involved in a peculiar dream of crashing aircraft flown by ants.

'Hugo! Hugo!' Jane's voice had a strange urgency.

'Okay, okay,' he grumbled resentfully. 'I'm awake! I'm awake!'

He pushed himself into a sitting position.

'Something's wrong, Hugo. I heard one of the workers wake Senhor Xavier and there is a great deal of shouting going on.'

'Right!'

Hugo, still moving in a semi-sleep, slipped from the bed and grabbed at his dressing gown.

He was halfway towards the door when he became fully awake.

'Jane . . .?' he swung round uncertainly.

She came towards him and kissed him softly on the mouth.

'Good morning, darling,' she whispered.

He smiled back and was about to say something, he felt the need to make some justification of his seduction of the night before but he found his ideas and thoughts lame in their formulation.

The sound of shouting made his head jerk up.

'You best go, love,' advised Jane. 'Xavier may need help.'

Hugo raced down the corridor to his own room, pausing to slip into jeans and a sweat shirt.

Xavier and Lopez were standing on the verandah looking towards the outbuildings where several of the indian workers lived in a large bunk house. Kanaraté and two other indians were standing by the verandah steps.

'What's up?' demanded Hugo.

Xavier's face was ashen. He made no reply but merely pointed towards the buildings.

For the first time Hugo became aware that one of the buildings was a different colour to the others; strange he had never noticed it before. Whereas most of the other adobe style outhouses were yellowing white in colour, this building, the main bunkhouse, was a reddy black colour. Hugo frowned.

Then his breath left him in a surprised whistling sound.

The walls and roof of the reddy black building were pulsating and changing shape.

He turned to look in horrified puzzlement at Xavier.

It was Kanaraté the indian foreman who spoke.

'*Formiga-de-correição*, senhor.'

'The ants!' confirmed Lopez in a whisper, terror edging his voice. 'Soldier ants!'

The group stood as if turned to stone. Hugo could hear faintly a discordant yelling and screaming. It was very muffled and accompanied by a banging sound.

Hugo felt the nausea catch at his throat as he realised that underneath that pulsating reddy black mass there were men still trapped in the bunk house.

Even as he looked he saw the door of the bunk house swing open, a man stand hesitantly on the threshold. Hugo registered every detail of the indian's terrified face. Then the door was slammed shut behind him to prevent the ants getting in. The indian began to move forward but already his body was acrawl with the reddy black insects.

The man waved his hands wildly to dislodge them, screaming now in agony. He moved a few paces, like someone trying to run through cotton wool. Then he was down and there was only a grotesque mound of pulsating reddy black to show where he had fallen.

'Sweet Jesus!' exclaimed Hugo, his voice hardly above a whisper. 'It's just not possible!'

Xavier, who had been standing like a statue, was now galvanised into action. He raced back into the house to re-emerge within a few seconds carrying a shotgun.

'That's no use, senhor,' cried Hugo, 'you can't shoot a swarm of ants . . . there must be some way we can help the poor devils inside the bunk house.'

Xavier eyed Hugo grimly.

'It is not my intention, Hugo, to shoot at the swarm. This is the only way we can help those poor men.'

Puzzled, Hugo and the others watched him.

At the side of the bunkhouse stood a big petrol tanker in which fuel for the plantation's aircraft was transported down to the airstrip. Xavier had seen it parked by the bunkhouse on the previous evening and had meant to tell Kanaraté to sack the driver for his stupidity in parking it so near the living quarters. But in the drama of the previous evening he had forgotten all about it.

Now Xavier raised his shotgun towards the tanker's side and, before Hugo or the others could completely understand his intentions, he let fly with both barrels. The pressure in the tanker caused tiny streams of petrol to jet out over the reddy black mess on the bunkhouse. It stirred uncomfortably.

Xavier bent the gun and inserted two more cartridges.

'What are you doing, senhor?' cried Hugo aghast. 'That petrol could go up at any moment!'

Xavier snapped the breech of the gun and raised it again.

'That is my intention, Hugo,' he said softly.

Twice more he fired while Hugo looked on in disbelief.

'Senhor . . .' it was Kanaraté. His face was pale. 'The men . . . the men in the bunkhouse.'

Xavier turned steely eyes to the indian foreman.

'What hope is there for those men in there, Kanaraté? Listen.'

Hugo suddenly realised that the screams and the shouting were dying away. Only one or two muffled sounds came from the building.

Xavier turned back to his task.

'There was no way we could have saved them. Now we have to save ourselves.'

He put down the gun and took out his silver cheroot case. Carefully he took out a cheroot and lit it. Then, slowly, he began to walk towards the bunkhouse.

Hugo heard a sharp intake of breath behind him. Jane, clutching Chuck, Conseulo and the housekeeper, Takky, had gathered behind the men on the verandah.

'What is the fool doing?' demanded Conseulo, gesturing at Xavier. Then her eye caught at the bunkhouse. 'What is that . . .?'

Her voice cut off abruptly as she recognised what was happening. A hand sped to her mouth to stifle a scream, her eyes rolled back and she collapsed onto the boards of the verandah.

'Take her inside, Lopez,' said Hugo without taking his eyes off Xavier's back.

The plantation owner was walking forward nonchalantly smoking his cheroot as if out for an afternoon stroll.

Suddenly Hugo started forward.

'*Vigia, Senhor!* Look out!'

A red-black arm had started to extend from the main body of the ants, sweeping slowly round in a semi-circle to the flank and rear of Xavier. It seemed incredible: the ants appeared to be aware of his approach and were moving to encircle and cut him off.

Xavier caught sight of them, waved his acknowledgement to Hugo, then took his cheroot from his mouth and threw it towards the bunkhouse.

Then he was running swiftly back to the main house.

For two long seconds nothing happened and then there was a tremendous whoosh! Flames leapt and danced over the building, engulfing not only its structure but the tanker as well.

The red black mass disappeared in a sheet of shooting flames.

Xavier came panting back to the verandah.

'Back!' he snapped. 'Back into the house, everybody! Lie down! That tanker is still full enough to blow us sky high!'

They pushed back into the house and threw themselves prone on the floor.

A second or so later came a roaring explosion, the crash of breaking glass as bits of metal and wood were thrown through the windows.

There was an eerie silence.

Hugo raised his head from the debris.

Xavier was climbing to his feet dusting his knees.

'Is everyone all right?' he asked anxiously.

A loud peal of laughter echoed round the room.

Conseulo, covered in dust and debris, was sitting on a couch giggling hysterically.

Xavier stepped forward and her giggling hysteria ended abruptly as he slapped her across the face.

'Look after her, Takky,' he snapped to the wide-eyed indian housekeeper.

'At once, senhor,' bobbed the woman, and led the sobbing girl from the room.

Jane was dusting herself down with a rueful smile while

young Chuck had already hastened to the window, eager not to miss any more of the incredible happenings.

Lopez was looking white and shaken while the three indian workers had gathered in a nervous group near the door.

Xavier joined the boy at the window.

The entire outbuilding system was now a sea of flames.

'Well,' said Xavier softly, 'no ant will escape that.'

He turned and laid a hand on the shoulder of Kanaraté.

'I am sorry for your colleagues,' he said simply. 'But they were already dead or as good as dead. You witnessed what happened when one of them tried to escape from the bunkhouse. It can be supposed that the same fate would have befallen all of them. We had to destroy the swarm before they could continue their destruction of us.'

He paused.

A silence greeted him.

'Do you understand this?'

The indians looked from one to another and then Kanaraté nodded slowly.

'It is as you say, senhor, though I lost my own brother in the flames,' said the old man.

Xavier let his hand fall limply from the old man's shoulder.

'I mourn for your loss, old man . . . as I mourn for the loss of them all.'

Hugo had been peering at the burning buildings. There was no sign of the ants.

'I guess you did it, senhor,' he said as Xavier joined him at the window. 'Looks like you put paid to them.'

'Thanks be to God,' said the plantation owner fervently. 'I hope the price was worth it.'

He gave a long sigh. Then he suddenly shook himself.

'We must be sure that we have destroyed the entire swarm.'

Jane cast a worried glance at Hugo.

'Do you think there might be some more about, senhor?' she asked.

Xavier nodded gravely.

'It is a distinct possibility. Think of the ant's productive powers and life cycle? Depending on the species, the ant has a life cycle of eight to ten weeks. During that time they can multiply themselves over a thousand per cent. And what is frightening, my friends, is the fact that we seem to be faced with a species of intelligent, thinking ant.'

Hugo found himself agreeing in spite of himself.

'Did you notice the way they seemed to know you were attacking them,' he asked Xavier. 'Did you see how they tried to cut you off and surround you? I've never heard of anything like it before.'

'Very well,' Xavier continued, 'we must form some plan of action. Lopez, I want you to get on the radio-telephone and see whether the electrical interference has abated. Try to get through to Morená and explain our situation here.'

Lopez pulled himself sluggishly to his feet. He hesitated uncertainly, then he nodded and went towards the study where the radio-telephone was kept.

Xavier gave an apologetic smile to Jane.

'I cannot allow you to travel into Morená today, Senhorinha Jane, at least, not until we have made sure that there is no danger along the way.'

'I understand, senhor,' nodded Jane.

'Most importantly,' said Xavier turning to Hugo, 'is the plan to ascertain whether this plantation is in any danger from any other swarms.'

'If only we had an aircraft,' said Hugo unthinkingly.

Xavier gave a shrug.

'It is my fault, I know. You told me often enough that I should buy a new machine. Nevertheless, we still have some vehicles. We, you and I, Hugo, must each take a jeep, divide the plantation into sectors and examine the area carefully. We must bring in all the remaining workers on the plantation to the main compound just in case. I think the main house will be the safest place in case of any more . . . er, disturbances.'

'Is there anything I can do, senhor?' asked Jane.

Xavier flashed her a look of gratitude.

'Perhaps . . . Hugo and I will take two of the indians,' he motioned to the men. 'But I will leave Kanaraté and Lopez here. I want you to organise a constant watch of the surrounding territory just in case we miss a swarm. See what can be done by way of defence. If there are other swarms about which are likely to attack us, we must devise ways and means of protecting ourselves.'

Jane nodded her agreement.

'I'll do my best. How long do you think you'll be . . .?'

Xavier hunched his shoulders.

'It is impossible to say, senhorinha. But we will try not to be long, eh?'

Lopez re-entered the room.

'Did you get through?' asked Hugo.

'No, devil take it!' grumbled the man.

'Still the static interference?'

Lopez threw himself into a chair.

'There is extreme static. You just cannot hear a thing. It would be better if we just got into the cars and made for Morená.'

Xavier straightened his back a little.

'This is my plantation, Lopez. I am responsible for all the lives on it. If the plantation is being attacked by these ant swarms, then it is my duty to protect it and my workers.'

Lopez gave a thin lipped sneer.

'As you demonstrated this morning, senhor?'

Xavier flushed and took a quick pace forward. His fists were clenched tightly. Hugo laid a restraining hand on the plantation owner's arm.

'Senhor Xavier did what had to be done, Lopez,' he said evenly. 'The men were already as good as dead. We know that. And had the ants not been destroyed they would have turned and attacked us.'

Lopez gave a shrug of indifference.

'No one will go into Morená until I say so,' said Xavier firmly. 'The safety of the plantation and the lives on it are of prime importance. Hugo and I are going to take the two jeeps and search the plantation in case there are other swarms. In the meantime I am leaving you, Lopez, with Kanaraté to help Senhorinha Jane to prepare the house against emergencies. Do you understand?'

Lopez' mouth twitched as he raised his eyes to meet Xavier's cold grey ones. It was Lopez who dropped his gaze first and nodded.

'Very good,' sighed Xavier. 'Now, Hugo, let us go.'

Hugo gave Jane a smile of encouragement and followed Xavier out to where the indians were waiting by the jeeps.


## CHAPTER FIFTEEN

Hugo braked the jeep on top of a knoll and took out his field glasses. Carefully he described a full 360 degrees before examining each section of the compass more slowly.

'No sign of anything, Kaluana,' he said to the indian seated beside him.

The man answered him with a nervous grin.

'Them devil creatures may be hiding,' he said suspiciously. '*Pajé*, him say, devil creatures sent as punishment.'

'What in blazes is *pajé*?' demanded Hugo, accelerating the jeep down the knoll towards the group of huts which housed the workers who tended the cotton fields.

'*Pajé* is *pajé*,' returned the indian simply.

'*Pajé?*' frowned Hugo. 'Oh, you mean a witchdoctor? Well, you don't want to believe all you hear, Kaluana. Anyway, what's he mean – the ants are a punishment?'

The indian held nervously to the sides of the jeep as Hugo bumped along the dusty track towards the group of huts which could now be discerned in the distance.

'*Pajé* say they sent to punish us. Sent by the Igaranhá because we deserted him and our gods, the gods of our people, and turned to listen to the blasphemous words of the *caraibas*' god Cristo. *Pajé* say we must return to the ways of our ancestors and make sacrifice to the Igaranhá and confess our sin.'

Hugo smiled.

'Sounds like your *pajé* is merely after converts. You don't want to believe in all that superstition, Kaluana. The ants are just normal living creatures whose behaviour patterns have gone a bit berserk.'

Kaluana shook his head.

'I do not understand, senhor.'

'There's nothing supernatural about the ants, Kaluana.'

He skidded the jeep to a halt in the middle of the huts and leant on the horn.

The place was deserted.

He blew the horn again. There was no answering sound save its echoes dying away across the hills.

Hugo shot Kaluana a perplexed look.

'They must have heard about the ants and left.'

Kaluana shook his head and pointed a shaking forefinger towards the corner of one hut.

'I do not think so, senhor.'

Hugo saw a white, glistening skeleton laying in a heap on the ground.

Cautiously, he climbed out of the jeep and moved towards the hut entrance. He peered into the gloomy interior. There was no one there. He moved on. In the next two huts there were five skeletons. In another hut he paused to be sick as his horrified gaze encountered a mangled, half eaten corpse.

'The ants have been here before us, Kaluana,' he said, returning to the jeep.

'It is as the *pajé* says,' whispered the indian. 'It is a punishment. We must appease the great Igaranhá for blaspheming against him. Only the blood of the godless will wash away our sins. It is as the *pajé* says!'

The man's voice rose to a shriek and he suddenly tore from his waist a long curved knife, similar to a Cuban machete, and raised it above his head.

Startled by the unexpectedness of the attack, Hugo threw himself sideways from the jeep just as the heavy knife swung down into the bucket seat where he had been sitting. It ripped open the canvas with frightening ease.

Still yelling, calling upon the gods of his tribe, Kaluana scrambled after the American, the machete swinging.

Hugo staggered to his feet just in time to see the downward stroke of the knife.

He lunged with his left arm and caught the indian's right wrist. Using the man's forward impetus, he sent Kaluana spinning over his thigh. Agile as a cat, the man was up again, machete still in hand, making short, vicious jabs at Hugo's body.

Hugo backed away calling on the man not to be such a

damned fool but the only answer was a cry to the Igaranhá to accept the white man as a sacrifice.

Hugo suddenly realised that he was fighting a losing battle. It was obvious that the indian was in better condition than he was, and that he was more used to wielding a knife than Hugo.

Reluctantly Hugo drew the Tokarev automatic pistol from his holster. He had felt it foolish when Xavier had advised him to wear it. What was the use of a pistol against ants? Obviously, Xavier had been wiser and he thanked God for it now.

'Put up your knife, Kaluana. I'm warning you, I shall use this if I have to.'

He flicked off the safety catch and levelled it.

Kaluana's answer was to launch a sudden, energetic attack which nearly caught Hugo by surprise.

The American depressed the trigger once, twice and then a third time. Red splashes appeared across the chest of the indian and the man sank without a groan.

For a moment Hugo stood looking down at the man. He was dead. There was no question of that.

Hugo swore loudly.

What in hell was this god-awful crazy world coming to?

Slowly he climbed back into the jeep.

Kanaraté had not practised his skill as a *pajé* or witchdoctor since he had come to work on the great plantation of the *Senhor de baraço e cutelo*. The missionaries, the *caraibas*, had come to his village when he was still a young man and taught him all the ways of their god Cristo. Kanaraté was impressed with Cristo, not so much by his teachings as by the wondrous things which he had given to his followers. They had carts that moved on wheels by themselves with great roars and snorting; sticks that spat flame and slew from afar; boxes that talked and even showed pictures; huts that rose up into the sky and were lost from sight and in which many tribes dwelt. There were countless other wonders too numerous to recall. Such were the blessings of Cristo.

Kanaraté, who had become a fully qualified *pajé* at the age of nineteen, was so impressed that he had turned his back on the Igaranhá and Jukuí, who ruled for evil and for good over the people of his tribe and, indeed, all the tribes of the river. As a follower of Cristo he had even turned his back on his village and, with his younger brother, set out to claim the benefits which Cristo could give him. He had come to the plantation of the great senhor to learn the ways of Cristo so that, in time, he, too, might possess the wondrous things which all *caraibas*, followers of the god, seemed to have.

The years passed. And now Kanaraté had spent over forty seasons at the plantation and was, by indian standards at least, an old man. He had never fulfilled his ambition for he found early on that even though the priests of Cristo taught all were equal before their god, it seemed that this equality only applied when men passed on to the spirit world over which Cristo reigned. Until one reached that spirit world there was a difference between all men; there were not just differences between the white followers of Cristo and the indian followers, between the black followers and those of mixed blood, but there were also differences in social grading between the white men themselves for it was taught that they must never mix together as friends nor marry women from each other's tribes. Indeed, the most generous gifts of Cristo were reserved only for the white man and for the highest class of the white men's society.

This Kanaraté had learnt over the years and it made him bitter and not a little ashamed of his rejection of the old ways and the old gods.

Was not everyone equal in the sight of Jukuí, not only in the spirit world but in this world as well?

Some weeks ago Kanaraté had heard it rumoured that the Igaranhá had finally tired of his rejection by the people of the river and was loose in the forest punishing all those who would deny him and the old ways.

And now Kanaraté had seen it with his own eyes: the hordes of the Igaranhá, the soldier ants who obeyed his words, were punishing the stupid, plump white followers of Cristo and all those of the people of the river who had rejected him.

That morning he had witnessed the end of his brother.

It was no less than a sign.

Now Kanaraté, squatting in his hut, had opened the canvas bag which he had not opened since he had arrived at the plantation all those years ago. In it lay his ceremonial emblems as a *pajé*: – the jawbone of his father, a string of beads from the pool where the spirit of Jukuí dwelt, some charms and some dried herbs. But these things he ignored. Instead he drew forth a great broad bladed knife, its once shining blade now speckled with rust.

Almost crooning to himself, Kanaraté the *Pajé* began to whet the knife on a handy stone.

There was only one way that the malevolent spirit of the Igaranhá could be propitiated: that was by the offering of the blood of the unbelievers, that blood being spilt by his hand as a token that he now rejected the evil into which the *caraibas* and their god Cristo had led him. He hummed softly to himself as he whetted the knife, working up the correct ceremonial from his half-forgotten memories.

When he had finished sharpening his knife he cast off his white man's denims and T-shirt and drew from his bag a skirt of *buriti*, fibre, and a feather headdress which perched atop the *Tavarí* mask of the water spirit, a hideous mask which covered his entire face.

From the door of his hut, at the back of the main house, he peered across the lawn to the verandah. On it he could see the figure of Lopez smoking a cigarette while sitting beside him was the senhora.

No, he told himself, these would not fulfil his purpose.

It was the Senhorinha Jane, the pale one with the golden haired head, she was surely chosen by the Igaranhá himself for the sacrifice; had not the Igaranhá woken when she and her father first entered the country? Was it not, therefore, her father and she who had stirred up the spirit's great wrath and had not the spirit already claimed the father? Surely, then, the Senhorinha Jane was the fitting sacrifice?

Yes: it was fitting. And he, Kanaraté the *Pajé* would be the instrument of the Igaranhá's revenge.

Unaware of two black malevolent eyes on her, Jane Sewell stood on the verandah and stamped her foot with annoyance.

'Listen, Senhora de Silva Xavier,' she said firmly, 'I am well aware that I am a guest in your house but your husband has asked me to help to clear things up and to organise a constant watch on the surrounding countryside. He also wanted the house prepared, if possible, for . . .'

Conseulo leant back in the wicker chair and blew smoke rings from pursed lips.

'Then, Senhorinha, it is a pity that my husband is not here to carry out his desires.'

'He told Lopez to help,' Jane gestured towards the man, lounging against the verandah porch, a cigarette in the corner of his mouth.

'Excuse me, senhorinha,' drawled Lopez, 'Xavier cannot tell me to do anything. I am no longer in his employ, remember?'

'I noticed you did not make that point when he told you to help this morning,' sneered Jane.

Lopez reddened and clenched his teeth.

'You forget yourself, senhorinha,' snapped Conseulo. 'You are, as you have confessed, a guest in this house. Hopefully, you will not be so for long.'

Jane turned on her heel.

'Little Chuck is up on the roof keeping watch,' she called over her shoulder. 'He is our only defence against a further swarm attacking us. I suppose it makes you feel better, Senhor Lopez, to let a child do the work you should be doing?'

The door slammed shut behind her.

Lopez looked after her and shrugged.

'Perhaps I better do something, Conseulo,' he murmured. 'She will only tell Xavier.'

Conseulo snorted.

'As you said, you have left his employ: are you so damned scared of him?'

'No but . . . but what if there are further ant swarms in the vicinity?'

Conseulo made a face.

'Of course there cannot be,' she did not elaborate on the logic at which she derived this decision.

'But in the circumstances . . .?'

Conseulo sprang up.

'The circumstances? The circumstances have made me realise one thing: I am leaving here, leaving this stupid plantation and its stupid problems. I am going back to civilisation. Xavier can carry on living here if he wants to but me, no thanks. I'm going back to São Paulo or maybe I shall get an apartment in Rio, civilisation with beaches, sandy shores, night clubs, anything away from this godforsaken hole!'

She had worked herself up into quite a temper.

Lopez looked on stoically.

'When will you tell him?'

'As soon as the stupid bastard comes back. I want a jeep to run me to Morená.'

'It's a long drive.'

'I don't care. Do you think I can stay another night in a place like this when . . . when . . .'

She gestured towards the burnt buildings.

Lopez was in many respects a weak man. That was why he was attracted to a self-willed woman like Conseulo, mistaking self will for strength of will. Oh, he could pretend to be dominant, he could mock her, laugh at her pretentious grand senhora ways as she tried to ape what she fondly considered gentility of breeding. But beneath it all he knew that it was she who dominated him. And now he felt frightened. Now he was without a job or position. And now Conseulo had decided to go back to the city where there would be plenty of men, rich men at that, flocking round her. He felt desperately alone.

He looked at her closely and, with a flash of intuition, she saw the desperation mirrored in his eyes. She felt a momentary surge of triumph.

'What . . . what about us?' asked Lopez.

Conseulo smiled. She loved the feeling of power over men.

'What about us?' she echoed, unable to keep the sneer from her voice.

'Perhaps we could make a fresh start together in Rio?'

She threw back her head and laughed.

'And give Xavier an excuse for divorcing me without a

penny, instead of me divorcing him? You must be mad. No, Lopez, Xavier is going to pay me, and pay handsomely. He will keep me in the style I've grown used to over these past two years of hell!'

Lopez let his jaw hang loosely so that he gave the impression of a small boy who had just seen his favourite toy confiscated as a punishment.

'But what of us?'

His voice sounded almost like a wail.

Conseulo eyed the man speculatively; she was unsure of her plans and she realised that perhaps Lopez would be needed in the future. He could be called upon for help, certainly she would need his help to get her away from this terrible plantation. Yes, she would need to play him along for a little while yet, this poor fool. She gave an alluring smile and reached out to take his hand.

'Of course I am thinking of us, Juan. Of course I am.'

There was a cajoling tone to her voice.

'You see, Juan, we must tread carefully, is that not so? We must beware of Xavier for he is very powerful. He will have spies in Rio who will report to him whether I am living alone or not. After we divorce, then that is another matter. In the meantime we must do nothing to arouse his suspicions.'

Lopez looked into her bland gaze trying to seek the truth behind her words.

'Juan,' her voice was soft but insistent, 'how can you think that I do not care about you after all we have meant to each other?'

She drew his hands up and placed them on her breasts, pressing them against the soft flesh and holding them with her own hands. Her head was tilted towards his, her lips apart and inviting.

Lopez was lost as he sensed the familiar stirrings of his body.

'Let's go inside awhile,' he grunted hoarsely.

A glint of triumph in her smile, Conseulo led him towards her bedroom.

Hugo swung down the eastern side of the cotton fields and

across the flattened track left by the ants. He felt somewhat dazed by the rapidity of events and was still not fully able to come to terms with the fact that ants could behave in the manner he had witnessed that morning. On top of that, Kaluana, who he knew had worked amiably for many years on the plantation, had suddenly gone berserk and tried to kill him to appease some old witchdoctor. Hugo shook his head in bewilderment.

He put the jeep into bottom gear and accelerated up a steep hill overlooking the trackway. This was where Xavier had informed him that a lookout had been posted to keep watch on the movements of the ant swarm. He did not even stop the jeep. The grisly white skeleton told its own story.

He swung the jeep round and back down the hill.

There was no sign of the ants nor the rest of the indian workers. A strange silence cloaked the forest, a silence which had hung over the Trumái village where he had met Jane. At least that was the one positive thing to come out of this weird business. Jane. He really felt all mushy when he thought about her.

He braked the jeep and sat for a moment wondering what to do next.

He had examined most of his allotted sector of the plantation. The workers seemed to have left it, or rather those who had escaped the devastation of the ant swarm. Also, Xavier's fears that there might be other swarms had proved groundless. There was nothing left to do but return to the main house.

He set the jeep in motion again, skirting the cotton fields and running back through the deserted collection of indian huts, the blood splattered body of Kaluana still lay where it had fallen. Hugo bit his lip and accelerated faster, swinging round until he came under the shadow of a large hill.

Abruptly he swung the jeep from the main trackway and followed a beaten path up the side of the hill as far as the vehicle could go. There was nothing wrong in taking one final glance round and Hugo knew that the summit of this hill gave a view for several miles.

Having left the jeep, it took him fifteen minutes of hard climbing to reach the granite top of the hill. He flung himself on the ground and lay on his back gulping the air into his lungs. Hell! Was he unfit! He silently swore to go on a crash diet and exercise to get his body in shape. He had had too much soft living and going everywhere in the bucket seat of an aeroplane. Maybe he should take up horse riding. He shook himself free from these inconsequential thoughts and climbed up to the highest point of the rocks and raised his field glasses to his eyes.

'Oh *Christ!*'

The words came out involuntarily. His nerveless hands let the field glasses drop and bang on their straps against his chest. Even with his naked eye he could see the great black strip, with its pinpoints of flashing red, as now and then the sun's rays glanced over the pulsating mass.

Slowly he returned the field glasses to his eyes.

About four miles off to the south, spread across the open hills almost as far as he could see, came a great black mass. The hills were covered. The front of the strip must be several miles wide at least and many times that in depth.

It was incredible! Preposterous! He was seeing things.

He swung his field glasses to the east but that section of the country was still hidden by the thick green rain forests. To the north there was nothing; no, not quite. He could see several black patches between the clumps of forests and the big rolling hills. He turned westward and again caught his breath. More black strips were covering the hills.

He sat down suddenly on a rock.

His hands were trembling and he had broken out into a cold sweat.

'I don't believe it,' he whispered to himself.

With studied casualness, he forced himself to stand up and examine once again the surrounding hills. At their nearest point the ant columns were four miles away but moving very slowly, relentlessly towards the plantation. There must be millions of them. And the plantation was surrounded.

Something seemed to snap in Hugo's mind.

The next minute he found himself running down the hill in a panic. He tripped, fell, rolled over, picked himself up again, tripped again, and it was a miracle that he reached the parked jeep with no more serious injuries than minor cuts and bruises.

He leapt into the driving seat, cursed when the starter did not fire the first time, nearly flooded the carburettor with the choke and finally got the vehicle moving, sending it flying dangerously down the rough trackway to the valley road.

## CHAPTER SIXTEEN

'Are you all right, Chuck?' called Jane, standing at the base of a ladder which led from the kitchen to the flat roof of the house.

The small brown face of Uuatsim of the Trumái smiled down at her.

'Yes, Senhorinha Jane.'

'Keep a sharp look out, then. Sing out if you see anything.'

The boy nodded his assent and returned to his post.

In the kitchen Tacuavecé, Takky the housekeeper, was piling up all the emergency tinned foods in accordance with Xavier's orders. The old woman smiled at Jane.

'How is it going, Takky?' asked the English girl.

'I have nearly finished, Senhorinha Jane,' said the woman. 'Then I must make sure that the fresh water tanks are filled from the well.'

Jane paused for a second and let some uncharitable thoughts fill her mind about Conseulo and Lopez.

'Perhaps I can do that?'

The old woman looked dubious for a moment and then smiled her gratitude.

'I would be grateful, Senhorinha Jane. It is a simple matter really. Buried beneath the house is a two hundred gallon tank for fresh water. The tank is supplied from a well about fifty yards away from the house. Senhor Xavier's father, who I served in my younger days, had an electric pump installed at the well which pumped the water along some pipes into the tank.'

'How do I do that?'

Takky took Jane to the kitchen window and pointed to the well.

'You will see a box beside the well head which is, as you see, bricked over. Here is a key to that box. All you have to do is open it. Instead you will see a switch which will start the electric motor. Switch on, leave it for perhaps two minutes until a green light above the switch comes on. Then you will see another switch under a dial. This switch you may then turn full on and this starts the pump. The dial will indicate how full the tank is.'

Jane took the key.

'Fine. It seems simple enough.'

She went out of the kitchen door and down towards the well head.

Kanaraté the *Pajé* lay beneath some bushes clad in his ceremonial clothes and clutching his long silver-bladed knife.

He had witnessed Lopez and the senhora leave the verandah with a sigh of satisfaction. Now if only the blonde-haired woman would come out, then he could make his sacrifice to the Igaranhá and save the Trumái from the punishment of the gods.

A faint bang, a door slamming against a wooden jamb, caused him to raise his head. Someone had come out from the kitchen door on the far side of the house.

Quickly, Kanaraté wriggled his way to the end of the building and peered round the corner.

His breath whistled through his teeth in delight as he saw the graceful figure of the blonde senhorinha crouching by the well head obviously working the water pump he knew to be there.

The gods of the Xingu were with him!

Silently, serpent like, Kanaraté eased himself along the ground, holding the great knife before him. Jane had her back towards him and was bent over the electric pump controls, face intent on the dial as its hands registered the flow of water into the tank.

The roar of a jeep skidding to a halt in front of the house sent Kanaraté headlong into the undergrowth.

123

The girl swung round and frowned.

Kanaraté lay flat on the ground, his weapon ready, but the girl had not even heard him. Her face was turned towards the house. She bent down and quickly flicked off a switch and hurried towards the building. The arrival was that of Senhor Xavier and Kanaraté cursed long beneath his breath.

Xavier was alone, his face creased in pain and there was blood on his sleeve.

'What has happened, senhor?' asked Jane, observing the apprehension in his face.

'Has anything happened while I was gone?' There was anxiety in his voice.

'Happened?' echoed Jane, sounding stupid. 'No . . . but why . . .?'

Xavier gave a groan, clutched at his arm and nearly fell.

Calling to Takky, Jane led him to a wicker seat on the verandah. Takky appeared and took charge, tearing his shirt sleeve from his arm and revealing a vicious knife wound. She brought a bowl of warm water and lint and began to bathe and dress the wound while Jane handed Xavier a glass of brandy.

'It was Sinaá, the indian who went with me,' explained Xavier. 'He suddenly drew a knife on me, telling me that his *pajé* had told him to kill all the followers of Cristo . . . he meant all Christians, senhorinha,' he added unnecessarily.

Takky started up with a hissing of breath.

'What do you know of a *pajé* on the plantation, Takky?' Xavier gave her a steely look.

'Nothing, senhor,' said the woman, indignation toning her voice. 'Am I not a follower of Cristo myself? I know no *pajé* man, no witchdoctor here, senhor.'

Xavier grunted.

'I thought we had rooted out all their mumbo-jumbo long ago,' he muttered. 'I've always tried to keep my folk clear of *pajé*.'

'What happened to the indian, Sinaá?' asked Jane.

Xavier shrugged.

124

'We fought over his knife. It was him or me. As it was he got in the first blow, Senhorinha Jane, but not the last.'

There was a grim satisfaction in his voice.

'I drove back here as fast as I could, just in case this *pajé* man was hanging around here . . . I can't think who it could be.'

He gazed steadily at Takky who returned his gaze coolly as she knotted a bandage in place around his arm.

'Everything has been all right here, hasn't it?' he asked, suddenly anxious again. 'Where's Conseulo?'

'I'm here.'

Conseulo, her hair ruffled and, to the discerning eye, a trifle breathless, leant against the kitchen door.

'And where's Lopez?' demanded Xavier suspiciously.

'How would I know?' said Conseulo, putting a cigarette into her sulky mouth.

Xavier suddenly banged his undamaged hand in anguish on the table.

'If the *pajé* man was here he would have shown himself while we were away. If he meant to kill us all, as Sinaá tried to kill me, he would hardly have let the opportunity go by when Hugo and I were gone. But as he has not . . . Great God! Perhaps the *pajé* man is Kaluana?'

Jane felt the colour drain from her cheeks.

'Hugo!' The word was torn from her lips. 'Hugo is in danger!'

Xavier had gone into the kitchen and was already climbing up the ladder to the roof.

'Do you see anything, Uuatsim?' he demanded of the boy.

'Nothing, senhor.'

'There is no sign of Senhor Hugo or his jeep?'

'No, senhor.'

Xavier climbed onto the roof and swept the horizon with his field glasses. Then he cursed and climbed down to face a pale-faced group of people who gathered in the kitchen. Lopez, his eyes downcast, had joined them.

'If Hugo is not back within the hour I shall go out after him,' announced Xavier, addressing himself to Jane.

'I'll come with you,' the girl replied.

'And what about me?' demanded Conseulo in a shrill voice. 'Am I to be left here with an insane indian about the place who wants to kill me?'

'There will be other people here, Conseulo,' there was a slight sneer to Xavier's voice. 'You are always thinking of yourself.'

'No one else seems to,' retorted the girl. 'I want to go into Morená when Lopez drives in. I am not staying here any more.'

Xavier met the blow without even flickering an eyelid.

He breathed deeply for a moment and then drew back his lips in a parody of a smile.

'By all means go, if you so wish. But there will be no driving into Morená until Hugo gets back.'

Abruptly, a frown chased itself across Xavier's brow.

'Where is Kanaraté? Didn't I leave him here with you?'

Jane shrugged her shoulders.

'I haven't seen him for some time.'

Lopez chewed at his lower lip.

'You don't think that Kanaraté could be this witchdoctor fellow, do you?'

Xavier gave a grimace which was meant to be a smile, but he was obviously in pain from his arm.

'Kanaraté has worked on this plantation for as long as I can remember. He worked for my father before me and has been one of the leading members of the indian Christian congregation. Kanaraté as a witchdoctor? If I am sure of one thing, it is that Kanaraté . . .'

The door suddenly swung open. Kanaraté, now clad in denim pants and a T-shirt, entered.

'Excuse me, senhor, I was busy seeing what livestock were still alive. A great many of our animals have been killed . . .'

The man hesitated as he looked at their grim faces.

'Kanaraté,' began Xavier, 'there is a *pajé* on the plantation.'

The indian's expression did not flicker.

'Impossible, senhor. We are all followers of Cristo here.'

'I say it is not possible, Kanaraté. Sinaá tried to kill me this morning and, before he tried, he confessed that he had been ordered to do this wicked deed by his *pajé*. He told me that all the white people were to be sacrificed to the Igaranhá. Have you heard of a *pajé* on the plantation?'

Kanaraté's face bore an expression of simulated horror.

'For longer than I can recall I have followed the teachings of the white god Cristo,' he said slowly. 'No, senhor, I know of no *pajæ* man here. But Sinaá had not worked on the plantation as long as three dry seasons . . . perhaps he was the *pajé* man who sought to reintroduce the old ways.'

Xavier shook his head firmly.

'No. Sinaá was a mere tool of the *pajé* man. Of that I am sure. He said as much before he died. But . . . but come to think of it, Kaluana joined us at the same time as Sinaá . . . perhaps . . . God, I hope Hugo is safe!'

'Shall I go and look for the senhor?' asked Kanaraté blandly.

'No. You relieve young Uuatsim on the roof. Keep a sharp look out.'

'Very well, senhor.'

The indian climbed up the ladder to the flat roof leaving a worried group below him.

'What can we do?' asked Jane. She wrung her hands agitatedly.

Conseulo was lighting another cigarette.

'Don't worry, your lover boy is old enough to look after himself.'

Jane opened her mouth to retort but merely shrugged.

'I apologise, Senhorinha Jane, for my wife's lack of manners,' said Xavier coldly. 'We must wait a while. If he is not here soon I shall go and look for him.'

Lopez was pouring himself a glass of brandy.

'I thought you were going to pick up the indian workers and bring them in to the protection of the main house,' he said, a touch of irony in his voice. 'Or has the talk of witchdoctors put you off?'

Xavier shot Lopez a look of dislike.

'There are no indian workers to be brought in, Lopez,' he said heavily. 'Most of them are dead. If any are left alive, they must have left the plantation. There are no signs of any survivors, only a few skeletons.'

'Oh shut up talking about it!'

It was the shrill voice of Conseulo.

'God! I want to leave here and I want to leave here now! Do you hear me, José? Now!'

'You'll leave when I say, Conseulo, and not before,' returned Xavier quietly. 'We have only one vehicle at the moment and I shall want to keep that until I am sure it is not needed. Is that clear? Now I suggest you go to your room and lie down until you can make a useful contribution to the company.'

His voice was soft but there was iron in it.

'Senhor! Senhor!' Chuck scrambled down the ladder into the kitchen. 'Senhor, there is dust coming along the trail. It is Senhor Hugo, I think.'

With a small cry, Jane swiftly climbed up onto the roof and, shading her eyes, she could make out a cloud of dust, in front of which she saw the form of a jeep, tearing along the trackway towards the house. There was only one man in the jeep. A white man. It was Hugo.

## CHAPTER SEVENTEEN

Hugo skidded the jeep to a halt before the anxious group of people and jumped out. He gave Jane a smile of reassurance and grasped her outstretched hand and squeezed it.

'Are you all right?' she looked wonderingly at his bruised and bedraggled appearance.

'Sure I am.'

Xavier stepped forward with a frown.

'Where's Kaluana?' he demanded.

'He tried to knife me . . . I told him to back off but in the end I had to shoot him.'

Xavier sighed.

'Damned native witchdoctors! Still, at least you are safe. Sinaá tried to get me as well. Apparently they still followed the Igaranhá cult . . .'

Hugo interrupted him with a wave of his hand.

'I'm afraid there's something more important, senhor . . . we've got to get the hell out of here; and *now*!'

Xavier's eyes narrowed and there were several exclamations and questions from the group.

'What is it, Hugo?' he asked evenly.

Hugo told them.

'There are more damned ants coming than you have ever dreamed existed in your life.'

'Where are they now?' gasped Jane.

'They're coming in on three sides of us . . . to the south, west and north. There must be millions – billions of them – moving on a front several miles wide.'

'I want to go, I want to leave now! Do you hear José?' Conseulo was hysterical and she started to sob without control.

Takky moved forward and placed a broad arm around the girl.

Lopez was swearing under his breath.

'Can we see them from here?' asked Xavier.

Hugo shook his head.

'We're too low down but I reckon the main contingent is about four miles off but moving fairly rapidly in this direction. The other columns, to the west and the north, are much further away but are swinging in a sort of pincer movement.'

Xavier stood with his head bowed.

'Very well, Hugo, I think we shall have to abandon the plantation. There is no way we can get through to Morená by radio. We'd better get out ourselves.'

'But if the ants are encircling us,' said Jane agitatedly, 'how are we going to get through?'

'I have a small cabin cruiser in a boathouse down by the river,' replied Xavier. 'Before the days of the aeroplane, the river was our only means of communication and sometimes it is still the cheapest way of moving supplies down from Morená. I keep the boat there and we have a straight through trackway from here. It's about nine miles from here.'

Hugo nodded.

'In that case, senhor, I guess we better start immediately.

There's no telling what these damn things will do next. Lopez and I will get the jeeps filled up with gas while you get everyone together. How many are we?'

'Only eight all told,' returned Xavier. 'Everyone else has either gone or perished.'

'Very well, senhor. I'll drive the leading jeep with Jane, Chuck and Kanaraté. You follow on with the others.'

'Right.'

While Hugo and Lopez filled the jeeps from the main petrol tank, a large underground tank which stood about a hundred yards at the back of the main house and supplied the plantation with fuel for all its vehicles, Xavier ran through the house trying to seal the place up so that the ant armies would not find an easy ingress into the building.

Each member of the party grabbed some personal possession which they wished to save. Xavier had to remonstrate with Conseulo who was demanding that she be allowed to take two suitcases containing her clothes and jewellery. Finally, after many tears and a screaming fit, she climbed sulkily into the second jeep clutching a vanity case in which she had stuffed a large quantity of jewels.

It was twenty minutes later when the two jeeps swung out from the main plantation buildings, turned across the fields towards a small stream and over a bridge which saw the commencement of a sunbaked trackway heading towards the river where Xavier kept his boat.

The vehicles kept up a good speed although once or twice, where the trackway divided into other paths and spread across the plantation, Hugo had to halt for Xavier to give him directions.

They said little as the jeeps bumped along the track, each were overcome by their own thoughts of the weird, horrific happenings which seemed like events out of some terrifying nightmare.

Soon the trackway began to climb through some low hills, the road swinging first one way over the shoulder of one and then over the back of another hill in a different direction.

Hugo, concentrating on keeping the bumping jeep on the road, at the same time with his foot hard on the accelerator, suddenly swung the jeep round a corner of a steep hill.

Then he was in a sea of reddy black and Jane was screaming hysterically.

'For Christ's sake, hang on!' he yelled, swerving the jeep into a tight circle, ploughing through the serried lines of marching ants, crushing them in their tens of thousands. The second jeep had stopped, its occupants hearing the commotion, and was now frantically reversing to find a space to turn on the trackway. Even over the noise of the shouting and the racing of the vehicles' engines came the hysterical peals from Conseulo.

Jane had now controlled herself and she watched in wide-eyed terror as Hugo, his face white and lips set in a grim thin line, managed to turn the vehicle out of the black mass into which he had driven. He swung the jeep in a semi-circle and, engine roaring, climbed up the hillside and back onto the track.

As brief as had been their encounter with the column of ants, the jeep was nearly acrawl with the creatures and Jane, Chuck and Kanaraté were busy swatting at the insects. They were about an inch to two inches long and coloured a cross between red and black, tiny vicious stings proved they were of a species which had a powerful sting at the tip of their abdomens.

The second jeep had turned by the time Hugo raced up to it.

'Did you see them?' he shouted at Xavier above the noise of the engines.

'Yes!' cried the plantation owner. 'How far do they stretch?'

'Too long a distance to drive through. We were almost covered by them within a few seconds.' He pointed to the squashed carcasses which bestrewed the jeep. 'Is there any way to get round them?'

Xavier made a negative gesture.

'This is the only trackway towards the river. There is another way, though, across the cotton field further north but it is extremely difficult country.'

'What have we got to loose?' yelled Hugo. 'Let's try that way. You lead off.'

Hugo threw the jeep into gear and set off after Xavier's vehicle, a swift glance over his shoulder showed him the incredible rapidity of the ants' advance. He shuddered involuntarily and then caught sight of Jane's pale, frightened face.

'It's okay, love,' he shouted, 'we're gonna be okay, d'ye hear me now?'

The two vehicles travelled rapidly over the dried fields which Xavier had been letting lie fallow for the year to rest the soil. They crossed a small stream without trouble and began to climb up a rather steep hill.

Hugo saw the leading jeep come to an abrupt halt on the shoulder of the hill and saw Xavier's shoulders slump over the wheel in resignation.

As Hugo roared up and halted his jeep alongside, Xavier picked himself up, turned and hunched his shoulders in a gesture of despair. There was anguish written in every line of his face.

'What is it, senhor?' demanded Hugo.

Xavier pointed down into the valley.

Hugo followed his extended finger and saw the familiar rusty black mass spreading along the valley floor and across the surrounding hills.

'It is no use, my friend,' said Xavier in a broken voice. 'No use at all. They are everywhere. We are cut off. Surrounded!'


## CHAPTER EIGHTEEN

They stood in a tiny knot by their vehicles, awe and horror fighting to gain mastery of their features as they stared at the black ribbons spread across the hills and valleys.

Hugo lowered his field glasses and turned to the ashen-faced Xavier.

'The damned things are moving more quickly than I

expected, senhor,' he said. 'There is no way through them or round them.'

Xavier sat with his shoulders hunched over the wheel of his jeep.

Jane, pale but resolute, held onto Chuck's hand while the boy regarded them with some sublime faith in his elders' ability to cope with the situation. Conseulo seemed to have fallen into some kind of merciful stupor, a state of shock, and merely sat in Xavier's jeep staring into space, a peculiar grin on her features. Takky, the indian woman, sat beside her, crooning softly to herself, reciting softly all the Christian prayers she could think of and when these were exhausted she prayed to Jukuí and every other spirit of goodness that she could recall from her youth. Lopez was muttering curses under his breath while Kanaraté stood a little apart, arms folded, an indifferent look having gained mastery of his features.

'Senhor Xavier?'

Hugo shook the plantation owner's shoulder sharply.

Xavier raised his head and let a sigh escape from his lips.

'What are we to do?' he asked wearily. 'If there is no way through them, nor round them, what are we to do?'

He sounded old and tired.

Hugo glanced at the group, his eyes coming to rest on Jane's drawn face. She tried to give him a brave smile.

'If we cannot go forward, senhor,' Hugo said, 'I suggest we return to the house, hopefully the ants have not reached there yet.'

Xavier was puzzled.

'Even if the ants have not reached it, they soon will. What then?'

'We have a good chance of defending the house from them,' Hugo forced an enthusiasm into his voice. 'We certainly can't protect ourselves here, but I think the house might have possibilities.'

He caught a glimpse of hope dawning in Xavier's eyes.

'I don't know what exactly you have in mind, Hugo,' said the plantation owner, 'but as I can't think of a possible alternative, you had better lead on.'

Once more the two vehicles moved off hurriedly, retracing their route back towards the main plantation buildings.

The nearest ant column was still well over a mile away as they halted before the house.

Hugo was out of the jeep immediately and issuing orders. Xavier made no objection to his taking charge.

'Jane, take Takky and Chuck down into the wine cellar . . . let Takky show you where it is. Get as many blankets, cans of food, torches and anything else you can think of which will be useful for a lengthy stay.'

Jane was already shepherding her party towards the house before Hugo had finished speaking. Conseulo followed them as if in a dream. She had still not recovered from her shock and was therefore useless. Jane let her go to her bedroom while she organised her working party.

Hugo was already up on the flat roof of the house, sweeping the horizon rapidly and then examining more closely the terrain nearer the house.

Xavier was looking at him dubiously.

'You plan that we should shut ourselves in the wine cellar, Hugo?' he asked, a somewhat incredulous tone to his voice.

'Only as a last resort, senhor,' replied the American. 'Your wine cellar is well built below the house. It is lined with thick stones . . .'

'Certainly,' interrupted Xavier. 'Except the roof, that is.'

'But from what I remember, the roof is covered with wooden beams across which is a tiled floor. There are two air vents and one doorway. In other words, senhor, it would be pretty easy to close the place so tightly that nothing could get in, wouldn't it?'

Xavier made an affirmative gesture.

'But then how would we breath?'

Hugo smiled as if that question raised no problem.

'It is not my intention that the last resort should be used, senhor,' he said, 'but the air vents are covered with a fine metal gauze which is mosquito proof and therefore ant proof. We should be able to breath quite easily. And surely no ant would manage to get through a six millimetre thick wooden door?'

Xavier scratched his head.

'Well, I hope we don't come to that last resort, Hugo. I think it's rather a precarious plan at best. It will depend on how long the ants take to pass over us . . . and *if* they pass over us.'

Hugo agreed.

'As I say, it is our final refuge if the other plan fails.'

'And what is the other plan? How do you intend to stop the ants?'

It was Lopez who interrupted, a slight sneer to his voice. But in spite of the sneer Hugo could read the look of fear in his face.

'Very simply. This house lies in a small valley, no? One hundred yards away on the eastern side of the house,' he pointed, 'runs a small rivulet. Just to the north is a dam which regulates the water here and provides the plantation complex with its electrical power via a generator just below the dam. The rivulet is also an aid for the irrigation system which Senhor Xavier's family built to provide water for the fields which immediately surround this house.'

Hugo paused and looked round their expectant faces.

'Therefore,' he continued, 'to the north a water ditch runs away from the river at right angles into the fields on the western side of the house. Similarly, there is another water ditch to the south, also running away from the river at right angles due west. Then, not more than seventy yards to the west of this building, these two irrigation ditches are joined together by a third connecting ditch crossing them also at right angles.'

He paused.

Xavier was looking puzzled.

'Well?' he demanded.

'In short, senhor, what we have here is really an island, albeit it two hundred metres square and only cut off by ditches with . . .' he counted, 'five, six bridges crossing the ditches.'

Xavier gave a short sardonic laugh.

'This is your protection?' he said. 'Listen, Hugo, those irrigation ditches are not more than four or five metres across. You don't think that these will protect you against the advances of a column of soldier ants? You know very little about them. Why, they have been known to pass over swollen, flooded rivers a mile wide! They use twigs, leaves, anything that floats. They are invincible.'

There was a dangerously high catch to his voice.

'Listen, senhor, said Hugo evenly, 'we really do not have a great choice in the matter.'

He gestured to the horizon where a tell-tale black line was emerging across the sandy-green hills.

'My plan is not merely the hope that the ants will march round the ditches if we pull down the bridges.'

'What then?' demanded Lopez. 'Do we start praying?'

'No. In a terrible way it was lucky for us that it was only the men's living quarters which were attacked and burnt this morning. The outbuildings to the north-east by the dam are undamaged. Senhor Xavier knows what's stored in them.'

Xavier scratched his head in perplexity.

'Dynamite, of course, but what else . . .'

His eyes suddenly lightened.

'Ah! I begin to see . . . you mean the storage tanks for the aeroplane fuel and oil?'

'Exactly, senhor. Firstly, we must destroy the bridges across the ditches, a charge of dynamite will do it quickly for us. Then we block up the ditches at each corner so that we have a continuous moat surrounding the house. Then we release the aviation fuel and oil into this moat. Should the ants really attack and begin to cross, we ignite the fuel. There is enough in the tanks to burn for a few hours at least.'

'Senhor Nosso!' exclaimed Xavier fervently. 'I think we begin to have a chance. The ants will have to march around the flames.'

Hugo was already pointing towards the horizon, the green of the hills were turning black as if someone had splashed paint across them and it was beginning to run.

'We must get a move on,' he urged.

Xavier nodded.

'You are in charge, Hugo. What do you want us to do?'

'To the jeeps. We'll go to the sheds and get dynamite

and shovels. Then we'll split into two parties. Kanaraté and I will block off the north, you and Lopez will block off the south. Then we will meet back at the fuel dump.'

It took three quarters of an hour for the house to become isolated by the destruction of the six bridges which led across the rivulet and the irrigation ditches. There was no time for finesse. Both Hugo and Xavier merely stuck sticks of dynamite under the bridges, lit them on short fuses and ran for cover. It was crude but an effective demolition and piles of splintered wood stood where the bridges had been.

Next, working rapidly and using the debris, the four men made makeshift dams across the irrigation ditches, piling in mud, rocks and whatever other material came to hand. The most difficult task was cutting off the rivulet so that the current swung round into the ditches to the south.

It was a race against time and Hugo more than once cast an apprehensive glance towards the advancing sea of blackness.

At last the temporary moat was ready and the four men met at the fuel dump near the small dam.

'How are we going to empty the fuel from the tank into the moat?' asked Lopez, frowning towards the great 300 gallon tank which had supplied the fuel for the plantation's single aircraft.

'By hose,' Hugo answered quickly. 'We'll place the hose into the northern irrigation ditch and let the oil flow round from west to east.'

'Will it work?'

'We can only try.'

There was a shout from the house.

Jane was waving to them. She turned and pointed towards the southern boundary.

The black mass was incredibly near.

Hugo cupped his hands to his mouth.

'Okay!' he called. 'Get back into the house!'

It was a matter of several long minutes before a suitable piece of hosing was attached to the valve at the base of the tank but soon the fuel was gushing out into the ditch.

'There's no need for us all to stay here,' said Hugo. 'Each man must make himself responsible for one of the sectors,

I'll take the northern one. Senhor, if you will take the southern one, Lopez can take the rivulet boundary and Kanaraté can take care of the western ditch. Make several torches soaked in fuel and if the ants start to cross throw them into the ditches.'

The others nodded and went off on their allotted tasks.

Keeping one eye on the gushing oil surging along the irrigation ditch, Hugo started to look round for some sticks and old rag which he could fashion into a torch.

A movement behind him caused him to swing round.

'Jane! What are you doing here? I thought I told you to get back in the house.'

'I thought I could be of use out here. Everything is prepared in the cellar. Chuck and Takky know what to do.'

'I'd rather you weren't here, love,' said Hugo, though without any degree of sincerity in his voice.

For a while they said nothing. Jane, seeing what he was doing, helped him gather some sticks and bind them into four torches which Hugo soaked in the fuel.

'Has Conseulo recovered?' he suddenly asked her.

'She has been hysterical twice since we came back,' said Jane. 'Now she's sleeping it off. I think it was more to gain attention than genuine hysteria,' she added unkindly.

Hugo climbed on top of the fuel tank and peered round the boundaries. He saw that the others had finished their preparations and were now standing waiting uncertainly.

To the south, the land was now black with the massing of countless ants. They seemed infinite in their numbers, relentless and ruthless as their broad fronted columns marched resolutely forward.

On the eastern and western boundaries the land was covered by cloaks of pulsating blackness.

There was a sudden gurgle and the pressure died from the hose. Hugo jumped down and looked at the gauges.

'Well . . . the tank's empty.'

He shouted the news to the others who acknowledged his cry.

Jane looked bemused and Hugo explained the plan to her.

138

'So that's why you were making torches? Will it work?'

Hugo laughed.

'That's the second time someone has asked me that question.'

He paused and looked serious.

'If it doesn't work, love, we're in trouble.'

He climbed back on top of the fuel tank and peered southwards.

Xavier was standing before the irrigation ditch, legs wide apart, an unlit torch in each hand. The black mass before him seemed to have stopped in its forward motion. It seemed at least ten metres away from the ditch, stretching away in a surprisingly ordered line.

Hugo turned to the other boundaries of the newly formed island. A cold chill went through him as he saw the land, almost as far as the skyline, black with the strange creatures.

Jane was looking up at him anxiously.

He climbed down again and gave her hand a reassuring squeeze but the apprehension in his face belied his gesture.

The great ant army had halted ten metres from the makeshift moat; had halted in a large black immovable mass. It seemed, incredibly, that they had sensed the danger and were now resting while their generals decided on the next moves.

Hugo looked from one boundary to another wondering from which section they would launch their attack.

'Hugo!'

Jane pointed frantically, one hand raised to stifle the scream that threatened in her throat.

A column, some metres wide, was moving swiftly from the main body towards the northern ditch. Hugo was still reaching for a match when the advance guard reached the ditch and, in spite of the thousands which perished in the thick, slimy fuel, many more were making their way over on twigs, leaves, even on the dead bodies of their comrades.

With a whoosh! Hugo lit two of his torches and reached to the ditch. He threw one at the crossing column and then, seeing another attempt being made further along the ditch, threw the other towards that spot. He had turned to light the other two torches when he realised that they would not be needed. Great tongues of flame were leaping in a solid wall along this sector and, when he turned, he saw that a similar thing had happened along the other boundaries.

The house was now cut off from the ant hordes by an impenetrable wall of fire.

He grabbed Jane's hand.

'Come on, let's get back to the house and see what's happening.'

Hugo and Jane began to run towards the house and saw Xavier, Lopez and Kanaraté following their example.

## CHAPTER NINETEEN

Night had come down with that suddenness which was typical of the dry season in the rain forest area. One minute it was light; the next a strange, pale gloom cast its warning shadows before the velvet blackness darkened the area. But the house and its remaining outbuildings were still bathed in light; the fuel in the makeshift moat still burnt, though not as fiercely as before, bathing the surrounding area in flickering red and orange colours. The heat and stench from the fire had a claustrophobic effect on the women of the party and the acrid smoke and smell of burnt aviation fuel and oil produced discomfort in everyone.

Hugo was sitting on the roof with Xavier peering around the house through field glasses which were fitted with night lenses.

He turned a troubled face to Xavier.

'It's simply incredible,' he whispered. 'They are still there.'

Xavier took the glasses from him and gave a quick, confirming search.

'It seems impossible, Hugo,' he said. 'What kind of intelligence must they have? Even I thought that they would have moved off once they were confronted with the fire. They have been there, still and waiting, for nearly four hours. It is horrible! Unnatural!'

His voice trailed off.

'That is the very thing, senhor,' agreed Hugo, 'we are dealing with an alien intelligence. More importantly, senhor, is the fact that my plan has failed. I thought that once they came to an insurmountable barrier, they would merely pass round it and leave us in peace. I underestimated their intelligence and their determination. The burning oil will only last until morning, if that.'

Xavier scratched his ear thoughtfully.

'So we will have to fall back on your last resort? We will have to barricade ourselves in the cellar and trust they do not find a way in?'

'I'm afraid so, senhor.'

A third shadow moved quietly on the roof top; it glided quickly to the ladder which led down into the kitchen and was gone without Xavier or Hugo realising that they had company during their discussion.

Kanaraté the *Pajé* halted with a thoughtful face at the foot of the ladder and stared unseeing round the deserted kitchen.

So the Igaranhá was invincible after all? His servants were waiting outside the ring of fire, waiting and watching, waiting to punish all these unbelievers for their desecration of the sacred forests and groves. Now all the followers of the *caraibas*' god, Cristo, were going to forfeit their lives for their brutal treatment of the people of the Xingu. Not only the *caraibas* were doomed but all the indians who had forsaken the ways of their ancestors to follow the *caraibas* and their god into slavery.

Kanaraté sighed heavily. What a fool he had been to think that he could become as rich as a *caraibas*. What a fool he had been to shun his people and the ways of his people to copy the ways of the white man, to imitate the white man even as the red fur howler monkey imitates the other denizens of the forest.

But Kanaraté was a *pajé*, a wise man of the Xingu, and in his old knowledge, though half forgotten, he realised his salvation lay in offering a token to the Igaranhá. By such token, when the silent servants of the Igaranhá swept over the house to devour its people, he alone would be spared, for he would have made his peace with the Igaranhá and the spirits of his ancestors.

He smiled to himself and nodded his head sagely.

Yes, he must finish what he had set out to accomplish that ·morning. He must offer up a sacrifice to the deity of the rain forest who had unleashed his servants against all who denied him. He must offer up the sacrifice of the fair-haired *caraibas* woman, the Senhorinha Jane, whose coming had marked the displeasure of the Igaranhá.

Jane Sewell must die. And die by the sacrificial knife of the *pajé*.

It was the will of the Igaranhá. Kanaraté knew it. In his mind he could hear a voice telling him it was so. No, not merely a voice, but many voices. Soft, high-pitched voices, voices like tinkling bells, like the rustle of the winds through the tallest branches of the rain forest, softly urging, pressing, exhorting and encouraging him to do the deed.

He stood staring, mesmerised by the voices.

He had never heard such voices before.

'What are you doing here, Kanaraté?'

Jane came into the kitchen.

Kanaraté shook himself.

'Senhorinha Jane . . . I was just getting some water.'

'Are the senhor and Senhor Hugo still on the roof?'

'I believe so, senhorinha.'

The indian watched her reflectively as she climbed the ladder to join the others.

A thought suddenly struck him.

He, Kanaraté the *Pajé*, had heard voices! The voices of the spirit people. Before this day it would have been a frightening thing. But now it only confirmed to him that he was a true priest of the rain forest gods; that he had been chosen to fulfil a sacred purpose.

He drew himself up.

It was surely a sign?

He turned and made his way out of the house towards the bush where, earlier that day, he had hidden his broad bladed ceremonial knife, his skirt of *buriti*-fibre and his Tavarí mask.

'Is there nothing else we can do?' Jane asked the two grim-faced men.

Xavier raised his shoulders in a gesture of despair.

'I'm afraid not, Jane,' confirmed Hugo. 'When the oil· burns itself out there will be no way to prevent the ants getting across to us. The only hope is to barricade ourselves in the cellar, block off all the means of getting in and out and wait it out.'

'What about air, though?' demanded the girl.'

'I've checked that. There's a couple of ventilation shafts covered with a fine metal gauze which is enough to keep the ants out but it will also let air into the cellar.'

'But what if the ants merely cover the gauze . . . you've seen how many there are of them . . . what if they block off these air vents?'

Hugo looked long and thoughtfully at the girl.

He could not confess that the idea had not even occurred to him.

'I don't think that will happen, Jane.'

Xavier opened his mouth to say something but caught Hugo's eyes and shut up.

'I wouldn't worry about things, Jane. We'll be okay.'

Jane wasn't convinced.

'Isn't there any other way?'

Hugo shook his head.

'It is so frightening. The ants just stand there in their masses and don't even try to get around the fire. What does it mean?'

Xavier laid a comforting hand on her arm.

'It means, Senhorinha Jane, that we are dealing with a highly intelligent species of life,' he said slowly. 'I am now inclined to agree with Hugo's theory that in some way radiation from the crashed nuclear bomber must have affected the metabolism and reasoning capacity of these creatures. They are a species of mutants, horrific as it seems.'

'But so many?' queried Jane.

'Ants breed fairly rapidly,' Hugo pointed out as he stood

up. 'Will you stay here and keep watch awhile? Xavier and I have to check the cellar. If you see the fires in any section dying down, just give a yell and hightail it down to the cellar fast. Got that? Not that,' he added hastily, 'the fire should die down yet awhile.'

Jane took his night glasses and peered out into the flickering red light.

'How long do you think we have?'

'I guess maybe until sun up.'

She smiled up at him.'

'Come back as soon as you can.'

He nodded absently and followed Xavier down the ladder.

Left alone, Jane gave a searching sweep of the flaming moat still spitting its tongues of fire into the black night sky. Focusing further, she could make out a surrounding black mass, here and there, as the firelight caught at certain points, there flickered a brilliant red light.

She gave an involuntary shiver.

Then, far away, she heard the distant murmur of the sea, pulsating with a slowness of rhythm which was quite hypnotic. She shook her head as if to clear it but the sound came again, louder, stronger.

The noise continued to grow in volume, then, through the whispering, she heard a high-pitched tinkling.

For a moment she was puzzled, then her heart started to pound as she realised it was the same sound that she had heard in her sleep walking nightmare.

She looked round, felt the hard coldness of the field glasses in her hand; felt the rough gravel roof; felt even from a distance the flickering heat of the fire. She was definitely awake.

The sea was murmuring with an intensity that almost hurt her ears. And through the sighing and ebbing of the sea came the tinkling crystal sounds which rose and fell, fell and rose, urging and enticing, imploring her to join them . . . To come to them.

Jane found herself standing up and taking one reluctant step towards the ladder.

Abruptly she swore, loudly.

She raised her hands to her ears and squeezed her eyes shut and kept cursing long and loudly.

The sounds abated.

Suddenly there was a silence again, broken only by the crackle of the distant flames.

Jane stared out into the night and shivered violently.

So it was *them*! They could communicate. They could mesmerise people. What terrifying creatures were they who had such a gift! Now she was sure that her previous nightmare was not the ramblings of her own imagination. Somehow those – those creatures – the ants – had induced her somnambulant state and caused her to walk from the house. As soon as Hugo came back she must warn him.

'Well,' she said loudly, 'I'll be on my guard against you now.'

Kanaraté the *Pajé* crept stealthily towards the house.

His body was taut as he prepared himself for his task. Long forgotten memories now filled his mind, soaking it with a hatred against the *caraibas*, the infernal white men, the never-ending source of all his people's ills. Was it not the *caraibas* who had brought disease, death and destruction upon the tribes of the Xingu? Was it not the *caraibas* who had provoked the dead spirits of their ancestors and the wrath of the Igaranhá? Well, now they were paying for their provocation, their puny lives were being eaten by the servants of the rain forest gods.

As he strove to recall the half forgotten rituals and lore of his people, the people he had turned his back on many years ago, Kanaraté recalled that in his tribe, at the age of puberty, all the boys had to go through a ritual before they were allowed to join the society of man. Most boys were circumcised, many had their noses pierced and were also subjected to ordeals by which they had to prove their courage and resolution. Afterwards they could sit in the councils of the men, talk equally with the forest gods and walk the strong hearted paths of the warriors and hunters.

The ritual of his tribe was being tied to a bed of biting ants.

A smile wreathed his face.

Why had he not thought of this before? This was why

the Igaranhá was sending his legions of ants to devour the unbelievers. Those who came through the ritual of the ants were to be born again as men and warriors who would walk in equality with the forest gods.

Kanaraté paused and fingered the sharpened blade of his sacrificial knife.

Well, he would not be found wanting.

He smiled as if a great weight had dropped from his shoulders.

He had been right all along. The ants were a plague from the Igaranhá. And it had been given to him, Kanaraté, to propitiate the spirits, to lay a gift of sacrifice at the feet of the gods and survive the ritual of the ants so that once more he could tread the path of equality.

He crept cautiously into the kitchen of the house. There was no one there but through the hallway he could hear sounds from the cellar. He turned uncertainly.

Then it was that he heard the voices again. Those soft, high-pitched voices, voices like tinkling bells, like the rustle of the winds in the tallest branches of the rain forest, softly urging, pressing and encouraging him.

He felt his footsteps guided to the ladder.

Ah, the fair one, the Senhorinha Jane. She was on the roof. Alone.

Breathing a special prayer to the forest gods, to the spirit of the Igaranhá, Kanaraté slowly climbed the ladder, one hand holding the hilt of his knife ready to strike.

Jane was kneeling on the roof, her back was towards the opening and she was gazing at the distant fires.

Like a snake, Kanaraté slid from the ladder onto the roof and crouched a moment in the shadows breathing deeply, his eyes on the fair white shoulders before him.

Raising himself, his hand held high before him, Kanaraté crept forward.

Some sixth sense at the back of Jane's mind caused her to glance over her shoulder at that precise moment.

She saw two bright pin pricks of light flickering from behind the dreadful Tavarí mask; saw the strange dark figure clad only in the mask and the *buriti*-fibre skirt; saw the fire reflecting on the sweat of the coppery arm and the silver flash of the broad-bladed knife as it began its descent.

She gave a long, loud scream and hurled herself to one side at the same time throwing the field glasses into the terrifying mask.

Kanaraté was aware that he had missed his downward lunge and caught his arm in its sweep, bringing it back, tensed again for a second strike. The field glasses crashed against his wooden mask, but, apart from stunning him momentarily, did not injure him at all.

Jane rolled across the roof before springing to her feet and facing the awful image which began to advance towards her again. Feet splayed out, arms akimbo, she looked hurriedly round for some weapon to defend herself with.

Kanaraté, arm upraised, moved quickly towards her.

'Help! Hugo! Help!'

Jane gave three piercing cries and moved backwards before the gruesome figure. She halted, aware that she was getting precariously close to the edge of the roof.

Kanaraté gave a hiss of elation as he saw that he had trapped her. Arm still upraised for the final blow, he now began to mutter an incantation to the great forest gods, formulae which he had last heard at the knee of the great *pajé* who had passed on his knowledge several decades before.

Jane, sidling along the wall, suddenly found herself in a corner of the roof. Her retreat was now completely cut off. The masked figure closed and she felt her muscles gradually becoming jelly as she watched the silver glinting of the upraised knife.

Then the knife was descending in an arc, straight for her chest.

She threw up an arm to defend herself.

In the distance came two bangs in rapid succession.

It seemed as if the masked figure had suddenly deflated like some balloon for the figure crumpled and the knife dropped with a metallic ring on the stonework of the roof.

Jane stared, her body quivering with the shock, looking down numbly at the huddled, grotesque figure.

Hugo was suddenly standing beside her, arms around

her heaving shoulders, murmuring gently in her ear, his lips brushing her cheek. She held tightly to him for a moment before regaining her composure and turning to look at the fallen body.

Xavier was bending over the figure.

'Who is it, senhor?' asked Hugo.

Xavier raised his eyes sadly.

'It is Kanaraté. He was the *pajé* who tried to persuade Sinaá and Kaluana to attempt to kill us. He was the *pajé* all the time. It is hard to believe. He was a Christian. He had worked with me for nearly forty years.'

Hugo sighed.

'You can never tell with these people. You can't expect them to become civilised in one generation.'

'That's unfair.'

It was Jane who spoke. Hugo looked at her in surprise.

'They have beliefs and rituals in which they believe just as firmly as we believe in ours. These terrifying happenings are enough to drive anyone to extremes.'

'You can say that after he tried to kill you?' asked Hugo in disbelief.

'You'll never solve problems by merely reacting to them,' said Jane. 'That's the trouble with mankind, action and reaction. No one ever troubles to think clearly about causes and make an effort to solve the cause rather than just eradicate the symptoms.'

Xavier knelt for a second longer looking down at the indian whom he thought he had known so well.

'I wonder what made him do it?' he mused. 'I thought he was one of us, not some savage still . . .'

'I could hazard a guess,' said Jane.

The two men looked at her curiously.

'The ants! They can communicate with us.'

'What?' Hugo gave a startled yelp.

'They have a sort of telepathic communication. You remember the noise and the voices that Chuck heard at his village and that I heard the other night?'

Xavier and Hugo nodded in unison.

'Well, I heard the same noise again tonight. It comes from *them*,' Jane pointed towards the fires. 'I don't know whether they can communicate with everyone, but certainly they nearly mesmerised me again.'

Hugo swallowed.

'The whole thing becomes insane. Mesmerism by ants!'

'Insane, but a fact,' said Jane. 'Perhaps they mesmerised Kanaraté?'

'We'll have to be on our guard then,' observed Xavier. 'You two had better get below and have some rest. I'll take over here for a while. Tell everyone to keep in the cellar. If the ants can mesmerise people by telepathy over a distance, we don't want people wandering about on their own.'

Xavier watched them climb down the ladder with a worried frown on his face.

He turned and peered down at the body of Kanaraté again, slowly shaking his head. Abruptly he bent, hauled the body into his arms and heaved it over the side of the roof. Then he settled down to watch the flickering fires.


## CHAPTER TWENTY

Conseulo gazed sulkily round the cellar from her perch on top of a be-cushioned packing case. Most of the occupants of the underground room were asleep. Conseulo's watch said it was nearly two o'clock. Only the Yanqui, Hugo, was on the roof of the house keeping a careful watch on the still-burning ring of fire. The men were taking it in two-hour shifts to keep guard.

Conseulo pouted in annoyance as she gazed at the sleeping faces of the rest of the little group which had been flung together in such horrific circumstances.

Why should they be able to sleep? she thought. How *dare* they sleep when I cannot? The pomposity of her ego made her fly momentarily into a rage but, realising that there were no witnesses to her mood, she immediately calmed down. With Conseulo it was self interest which had dominated her whole life. But that was understandable for a little girl who was left to bring herself up in the squalor and slums of São Paulo as best she could. It was a loveless life in which no one had really cared about her and in which the only way to gain attention was to do something extreme. Such a life had produced in her a grim determination to survive and to bend all things to her own self interest.

She had now recovered from her hysteria, her mind registering that such tactics were not getting her the attention she wanted. In the face of the danger from the ants, no one had been able to spare her the time to indulge her moods.

She gave an apprehensive shiver as she let her mind dwell on the ants.

Conseulo made no attempt to rationalise the situation, to reason it out. It was not in her nature to do so. She merely saw the ants as an extension of the suffering which she felt she had endured ever since she came to live with Xavier on his plantation. He cared more for the land and his crops than he did for her. Strangely, she did not blame him for not caring for her. No one had ever cared for her and there was no reason why they should. But Xavier had a duty to ensure that no wish of his wife's went unfulfilled.

Xavier should establish her in a nice apartment or a villa in Rio, not São Paulo, she decided. São Paulo carried too many unpleasant memories of her childhood although, in a perverse way, she would like to return to visit the hotels, clubs and bars where a few years ago she would not have dared to enter. She smiled with grim satisfaction at the idea.

No, Rio was the place for her. Xavier could have his rotten plantation, could live here if he wanted. In fact, better he live here. She could then live a free life, do anything she wanted, everything she had ever dreamed about as a child. Have lovers of her own age.

Her gaze came down on the gently snoring Lopez.

Lopez? She had no plans for him in her future world. Lopez had helped to prevent her boredom on the plantation, that was all. Apart from that fact, Conseulo regarded Lopez as she regarded every other man who came into her life. Men had used Conseulo and so Conseulo, in her turn, had learnt to use men for her own pleasures and goals. To suggest that there was any other form of relationship in life between men and women, that there *should* be any other form of relationship, was totally ridiculous. Conseulo did not admit of any other emotions, having stifled her own emotions in the unloving atmosphere of her childhood. Perhaps it was strange, therefore, that Conseulo's pleasures included reading magazine stories of the romantic type from which she derived some indefinable satisfaction from the dewy-eyed amours of the heroines.

She lowered her lids as she heard someone entering the cellar.

It was the lanky Yanqui. She felt a wave of intense anger as she regarded him beneath her lowered lids. He was an attractive man, certainly, and when he had first arrived at the plantation she had been pleasant enough to him and he to her. Even at that time she was growing bored with Lopez; Lopez, who in many ways was merely a handsome animal who had no illusions about Conseulo. It was nice to flirt with someone who had illusions.

She ground her teeth as she recalled the night she had gone along to the stupid Yanqui's rooms and offered herself to him, positively offered herself! He had smiled and firmly pushed her out, pushed her out and told her to return to her husband. What was he? A cabbage – a homosexual? No, there was something between him and that cold, blonde bitch of an English woman.

It had been the first time in her life that Conseulo had been rejected by a man and she had never forgiven him.

The Yanqui was leaning over Lopez and shaking him.

'Lopez!' his voice was an urgent whisper. 'Lopez! It's your turn for watch.'

Lopez rolled over and began to lever himself up yawning.

'What time is it?'

'Nearly two o'clock.'

'How are the fires?'

'Still burning, nothing can get across yet but I don't

reckon they can last more than another two or three hours.'

'And the ants are still there?'

'Yes.'

'Then what happens when the fires die down?'

'If they start coming across, then we shut ourselves down here and wait until they go away.'

Lopez gave a cynical laugh.

'And if they don't go away?'

'We're open to suggestions, Lopez.'

Lopez snorted in disgust, buttoned his coat, took the field glasses from Hugo and left the cellar.

Conseulo watched while Hugo looked round the cellar, moved across to the corner where the Englishwoman was sleeping and lay down close by. Conseulo's face creased into a contemptuous sneer.

About half an hour later, Conseulo stood up.

She was unable to sleep but, strangely, it was not the thought of the waiting ants that troubled her. It didn't really enter her consciousness that the ants were a threat to her, personally. She gave no thought to the peculiarity of the ants nor the terror they threatened. They were simply part of the grotesqueness of life on a plantation in the grim rain forests of the Matto Grosso. Following her hysterics, Conseulo had simply assured herself that she would survive as she had survived many catastrophes in her crowded life.

She accepted that Xavier, and the men with him, would be able to provide a means of dispersing these irritating insects and, having accepted that, her mind had flown to other things, more important things in her estimation, such as her imminent break with Xavier.

Conseulo stretched and drew a shawl around her shoulders. She cast a further glance around at the sleeping figures and then walked out of the cellar, up the steps into the kitchen. Here she poured herself a large whisky and stood sipping it. Through the windows she could see the flickering of the fires along the makeshift moat.

The scrape of a shoe on wood caused her to swing

round. Lopez was standing on the upper rungs of the ladder which led up to the roof.

He grinned down at her.

'So it's you. I thought I heard something.'

Conseulo gave him a calculating scrutiny.

'Want a drink?'

He gave a negative shake of his head.

'I've got to get back on the roof in case those fires die down sooner than expected.'

Conseulo, still clutching her glass of whisky, followed him up the ladder and out onto the flat roof.

It was colder than she expected and she drew the shawl tighter round her shoulders.

'How soon will it be before we can get out of here?' she demanded.

Lopez shrugged.

'It depends on these damned things out there.'

He raised the field glasses, with their night lenses, to his eyes and peered beyond the fires.

'I find it eerie. They just sit there, or stand there, whatever ants do. They just wait. Hundreds of them, millions of them. I've never seen anything like it before.'

Conseulo, imperturbably, took a swallow of her drink.

'Just so long as we get out of here soon. It's driving me mad, this being couped up. We should have driven on this morning and got to the river.'

Lopez did not bother to pursue the point.

Conseulo could be extraordinarily stupid at times, he mused, resuming his examination of the boundaries.

'Lopez,' Conseulo suddenly put down her glass of whisky. 'Make love to me.'

Lopez was taken aback at her abruptness.

'Conseulo . . .' he began.

'Here, Lopez! Now!'

Suddenly she was in his arms, her hungry open mouth tearing at his, her arms, her hands, clutching and demanding. It was as if she were attacking him. The thought registered in Lopez' mind. There was no emotion in her demands, no love, merely a physical need. A desire for animal gratification. He fell back on the roof beneath her weight. The impetus was all her own. Lopez lay in almost stunned placidity as Conseulo sought to fulfil her needs.

A sense of shame abruptly overcame him. This was no way for a man; it was not manly this thing; a woman should not be dominant in lovemaking!

Then his mind gave up, surrendering to the intensity of excitement and soon he had taken over the impetus of the struggle, soon they reached a climax and fell apart gasping for breath.

After a short while Conseulo stood up, straightening her clothes. Wrapping her shawl once more around her shoulders she bent and picked up the rest of her whisky, which by some miracle, had not been knocked over. She sat on the low parapet of the roof and commenced to sip it as if nothing had taken place.

A sense of sadness arose in Lopez' mind. Sadness tinged with guilt and frustration. Sex to Conseulo meant no more than eating a ripened orange, a sensual pleasure to be sampled, enjoyed at the moment and then forgotten. Sex was no more than that – no more than having a cup of coffee to fulfil a thirst. In the two years he had been Conseulo's lover he had never fully understood that as he did now. Never fully realised just how deep her selfishness went.

He began to feel a disgust with himself and turned away from her, pulling on his discarded clothes. One day soon they would have to discuss this relationship and he prayed he would be strong enough. He knew he was weak in the face of Conseulo's demanding personality but at least he had begun to recognise that weakness.

He did not know how long they sat on the roof without saying anything.

Suddenly Conseulo's voice was sharp.

'What did you say?'

Lopez glanced at her.

'What?'

His face was blank.

'Didn't you say something?' demanded Conseulo.

Lopez gave a negative gesture.

There was a brief, silent pause. Lopez was then aware

of Conseulo standing up, there was a tinkle of glass as her tumbler fell from her hand.

'Careful,' he protested.

Without a word, Conseulo turned and was going back down the ladder.

'Try to get some sleep,' Lopez called in a low voice after her.

There was no answer.

Conseulo stood in the kitchen her mind filled with the gentle rhythmic surge of the sea, the rise and fall of the surf crashing on shingle, the low soft intake of the undertow, the sudden surging and violent crash of the waves. It was hypnotic, soporific, soothing.

And through this gentle sound came the distant tinkle, like crystal blown by a gentle breeze, soft at first and then growing more insistent and louder.

It filled her mind with strange thoughts.

It called to her to go to meet it, to come to it and help it. Yes, it needed help. It wanted help immediately. It had to get over something and needed assistance to do so.

A vision of a wrecked bridge came into her mind. A small bridge across a six metre wide ditch. The ditch was filled with burning oil or something, but around the wreckage there lay long heavy timbers, blown there by some explosions. The voices, the tinkling crystal, wanted her to go and place the beams across the ditch of burning liquid so that they might cross it.

Conseulo tried to shake her head but the sounds had taken over her mind completely, cajoling, promising, imploring. She felt compelled to follow the urgings of the crystal voices as they clamoured into her ears, clamoured against the droning voice of the sea.

'All right,' she whispered, 'all right. I am coming.'

Lopez on the roof of the house suddenly noticed a flash of white in the darkness. He turned his field glasses towards the object.

'Conseulo!'

He frowned and then yelled as loud as he could: 'Conseulo, come back!'

There was no answer but the white material of the girl's blouse flashed again as the figure of Conseulo hurried towards the southern irrigation ditch.

Lopez' brow creased in disbelief.

Suddenly he was on his feet and scrambling down the ladder. The kitchen door was open.

'Conseulo! Conseulo! What the hell are you doing?'

His voice carried on the night air but the girl did not stop. She moved almost mechanically. She had reached the southern ditch, reached the spot where a small bridge had spanned the irrigation canal and which had been dynamited by Xavier earlier. Several timbers lay about and Conseulo was now bending down and tugging at them. She seemed to be tugging them towards the ditch.

Lopez reached the girl and swung her round by the arm, his face working in his panic.

'Conseulo! What in hell are you doing?'

The girl looked up at him and he was appalled by the blaze of hatred in her eyes. Her face was ghastly in the flickering firelight.

Lopez started back. He had never seen such a look of loathing on anyone's face before.

His hand dropped from her arm.

Suddenly she had swooped down, picked up a piece of timber and was whirling it round her head.

Lopez instinctively raised an arm as the timber descended towards his head.

There was a loud crack as the timber struck home against his arm.

A scream came from his mouth, there was a flash of blinding pain followed by a brief numbness in his arm. It hung limply at his side.

He had no time to think again for the timber was already making another descent.

He sidestepped just a fraction too late. The wood caught him a glancing blow on the side of the temple and he plunged into a blackness which was both deep and velvety.

He must have been unconscious for only a few seconds for the next thing he knew was a vague shouting from the house. In front of him Conseulo had succeeded in getting a long timber and was gasping as she pushed it across the ditch. Even as he scrambled to his knees, Lopez saw the end of the timber touch the furthest bank, saw that even while the flames licked hungrily around it, a small column of ants began to start across.

'Christ, no!' Lopez screamed. He ran to the timber and bodily threw Conseulo to one side. She fell to the ground and lay spitting venomous curses at him.

Lopez bent down and started to heave at the timber. Even with his mind in a turmoil he marvelled at the strength which Conseulo must be possessed of in order to have pushed it into place.

But the vanguard of the ants were across. They were leaping onto him, were crawling on his chest, his clothes, across his neck. He could feel their savage pin pricks, almost feel the individual sharpness of their teeth. Hundreds of them. Thousands of them. They were at his neck. My God! On his face! Crawling into his mouth, his ears, his nose, his eyes. The pain was intolerable. He raised his good arm to brush them off. He was covered. A small black shape. A parody of a man.

Screaming now, loudly, terrified, Lopez staggered this way and that in order to seek an escape from the mass which had engulfed him. Then, in a final frenzy of despair, he leapt for the burning fuel in the ditch.

Conseulo, her mind shaken from the strange somnabulant state, watched in horror at the still-living figure of her lover moving feebly in the flames.

Then the figure was still.

She could do nothing but open her mouth and give forth shriek after piercing shriek.

The column of ants, marching across the fire by means of the timber, losing many of their comrades enroute to both the flames and the heat, but pressing on in their thousand, reached her hysterical form. They swung round in a semi-circle as though to surround her. Still shrieking wildly, Conseulo dragged herself to her feet and started to plunge forward towards the house. Abruptly, she halted as she realised she was surrounded. Then, desperately, she start to run forward, run through the black mass now encircling her.

In silent horror, at the kitchen door of the house, Xavier and Hugo stood watching the gruesome spectacle in the light of a torch. Hugo sharply ordered Jane to remain below in the cellar with Takky and Chuck.

The figure of Conseulo, in red skirt and white blouse, suddenly became black as thousands upon thousands of ants leapt upon her running figure. They saw the figure wildly beating its hands, heard the terrified shrieks, saw the figure go down and within moments heard a loud, echoing silence.

Xavier leant against the doorjamb and was sick.

Hugo turned and dragged the plantation owner into the kitchen and slammed the door. The man was half crying and half laughing. Hugo reached forward and slapped him hard across the face.

Xavier looked up at him a hurt and bemused expression in his eyes.

'Senhor! Senhor!' urged Hugo. 'It's too late to help either Conseulo or Lopez! We must try to save ourselves! Do you hear?'

The plantation owner had suddenly aged. He looked about him in a dazed fashion.

'Do you hear, senhor?' repeated Hugo. 'The ants are coming! They have managed to get across.'

Suddenly Xavier's eyes focused and he opened his mouth but no sound came out.

Hugo pushed him across the kitchen and bolted the door shut. He could hear a peculiar rustling sound outside. He jumped to the roof and swung the trap door shut before taking down the ladder. The other windows and doors of the house were secured. He and Lopez had made sure of that earlier in the day. He turned. Xavier was still standing helplessly in the centre of the kitchen. He was crying softly. 'Conseulo! Conseulo!' It was the only word that made any sense.

The rustling noise was now very loud and seemed to be all around them.

Several ants had managed to come through under the door.

With a viciousness which surprised himself, Hugo brought his boot down on them but their numbers were increasing all the time.

The rustling noise was almost deafening.

Hugo backed down the cellar steps, pushing Xavier in and swinging shut the door. He secured it with bolts and then spent a few minutes placing reinforcements of wood across the door.

Finally he turned to the group of white-faced people who stood before him.

'Well,' he said quietly, 'they've come.'


## CHAPTER TWENTY-ONE

Six hours later the air in the cellar was stale and breathing was becoming difficult. The men had removed their shirts and the women, Jane and Takky, had unclothed as far as modesty allowed. Still the sweat stood out on their foreheads and they moved sluggishly.

Jane looked at Hugo and raised her eyebrows.

'It is as I thought, Hugo,' she said, pausing every few words to take in deep breaths. 'The hundreds of ant bodies pressed against the metal gauze of the ventilation shafts must have completely blocked off the air.'

'I was so sure they would move on,' he gasped. He spread his hands in a gesture of hopelessness.

'We must face the facts,' Jane insisted coolly, 'we seem trapped. The ants are not getting in, it's true, but then neither is any air. A few more hours like this . . .'

She shrugged.

Takky gave a small cry, grasped her rosary more fiercely and fell to reciting quietly until she gave up for want of breath.

Hugo shot a concerned look at Xavier.

The old man sat with his shoulders hunched, his arms clasping his legs, his head buried on his knees. He had uttered no word since Conseulo's death. Jane said that the plantation owner was in a state of shock. The boy, Chuck, thankfully was asleep.

'I suppose they are still out there?' whispered Jane.

Hugo's ears attuned themselves to the incessant rustling sound and nodded grimly.

'Yes,' he confirmed. 'It's my fault. I should have taken you seriously when you told me earlier about the ventilation shafts.'

Jane reached out a hand and squeezed his arm.

'You did your best, darling,' she said softly.

'Which wasn't good enough,' exclaimed Hugo bitterly. 'I should have tried something else. Maybe we could have burnt our way through them.'

'How?' demanded Jane.

Hugo raised his hands helplessly.

'I don't know. Somehow.'

Jane smiled sadly and shook her head.

'We'd better conserve as much air as we can,' she said. 'The ants can't get in and we can't get out, so it's a stalemate. One thing, we don't appear to be susceptible to their mesmerism treatment down here.'

'You really think that it is their form of communication?'

'I'm sure of it,' said Jane emphatically. 'I'm sure that's what happened to Lopez and Conseulo . . .'

'Conseulo?'

It was Xavier.

'Where's Conseulo?'

The old man stood up and looked round in bewilderment.

Jane bit her tongue. Hugo crawled over to the old man, and placed an arm across his shoulders.

'Senhor,' he said gently. 'Conseulo is dead. Don't you remember?'

The plantation owner suddenly collapsed into a fit of sobbing.

Hugo glanced at Jane helplessly.

With an almost uncanny abruptness the light started to flicker and then went out, plunging the cellar into complete darkness for a moment or two before Hugo found and switched on a powerful electric lamp.

'That must have been the generators clogging up,' he observed.

'Right now,' there was a sharp edge to Jane's voice, 'we must stop wasting oxygen. No more unnecessary talking or exertion. And pray that in the next couple of hours they decide to move on.'

Hugo came and sat by her and Jane let herself nestle against his shoulder. Takky was now quiet, cradling little Chuck in her ample lap and even Xavier seemed to have fallen asleep.

It was about an hour later when a faint booming sound caught their ears. Xavier sat up with a start and looked round in the semi-gloom. For about ten minutes there followed a series of muffled booms and thuds, and one strange-sounding and loud thump as if something had struck at the walls of the house. Then the noises ceased.

Hugo shrugged in answer to Jane's raised eyebrow.

The air was getting really bad now. Hugo glanced at his watch and then looked away self consciously as he caught sight of Jane's anxious face peering at him.

'To be honest, darling,' she whispered, 'if it's a choice, I'd rather black out and die through lack of oxygen than be bitten to death by those things out there.'

Hugo's face was grave.

'I think it's time for that choice, I'm afraid.'

'Then just keep your arm round me. We'll go to sleep and . . .'

'What on earth!'

Xavier had started unsteadily to his feet with an exclamation of surprise.

'Is it the ants?' snapped Hugo, struggling to swing the electric lamp towards Xavier's corner.

'No . . . no . . .' gasped Xavier, who seemed to have recovered his equilibrium. 'Shine the light over here, over here, quickly!'

Hugo swung the electric torch towards the spot Xavier indicated. The spot where he had been sitting was now swimming in water and several ants were floating in it on their backs. With a muttered exclamation, Hugo followed the line of water and found it entering the cellar in two respectable dribbles from the ventilation shafts. A quick examination from his flashlight showed the ventilators to be still blocked from the outside.

An idea began to form in Hugo's mind.

Gasping for breath he trod carefully, swaying like a drunken man, towards the cellar door and examined its base. There was another pool of water which was seeping steadily into the room from under the door.

He turned round and paused while he tried to draw sufficient breath into his lungs.

'I . . . I think . . . we may . . . be saved.'

He could see their incredulous stares in the light of the torch.

'Think . . . think . . . dam . . . burst. Whole area . . . flooded.'

Xavier was leaning against the wall, his mouth working for air.

'You . . . you mean when we made the moat . . . we blocked off the water flow . . . so no water flowing downriver passed the dam . . . we provided no alternative route for water . . . now river has burst banks . . . you think the whole valley round house is under water . . . that ants might get swept away?'

Jane smiled broadly.

'The noise . . . loud bang . . . noise of bursting dam?'

Hugo nodded vigorously, panting with the exertion.

'But how will we get out . . . if the house is under water?' asked Jane.

Xavier shook his head.

'River . . . river would not be able to flood . . . area in any great depth . . . two or three feet at the most. Enough to clear ants, though.'

Hugo drew himself up.

'We'll try to get out. All agreed? I want you all . . . over by the cellar door, all holding hands as fast as you can. Don't for God's sake let go. Jane, you stand directly . . . behind me, hold on . . . on to my belt . . . and everyone else hold on behind. I'm going to open the . . . cellar door!'

There was a tense silence as Hugo unbolted the wooden door. Even as he started to turn the handle he could feel a great weight pressing in on the door. Suddenly it flew back with a snapping of the lock, the force almost knocking him over and ill preparing him for the tremendous cascade of water which poured down into the cellar. Hard black things stained the water. It was full of drowned ants, and ants pressed into a messy pulp by the pressure of the water. Soon the cellar was filling up and the pressure through the doorway had decreased. Grabbing at the handrail of the stairway, Hugo began to haul himself upwards, glancing distastefully at the masses of insects that almost seemed as great in volume as the water.

It took fully fifteen minutes of gasping, pausing and hauling before the group were standing knee deep in water in the kitchen. They sprawled over the kitchen table, the only high, dry spot, in the room, breathing deeply and gradually recovering their breath while the awful polluted waters lapped lazily around them.

There did not seem to be a live ant left in the house.

Xavier was the first to recover and go to the kitchen window. What he had surmised was true. In their panic to dam the rivulet which ran north to south on the western side of the house, and create a moat, they had forgotten to provide an alternative route for the rivulet above the dam to the north. Gradually, over the hours, the water pressure had built up behind the dam until, with no other outlet available, it had burst the dam and the waters had cascaded over the valley floor washing away great sections of the ant army which had been smothering the house.

Those ants inside the house, those jammed against the ventilation shafts and the door of the cellar, their bodies used to prevent air entering to the besieged group, were simply crushed by the weight of water as it crashed in on them. Millions more had been drowned, while many others had been washed away to reform on the higher ground about three hundred yards away to the south and east.

The hills in these directions were still black with countless columns of soldier ants.

Hugo joined Xavier at the window and let out his breath in a low whistle as he examined the scene of devastation.

'We seem to have won.'

'It is only a temporary respite, Hugo,' replied Xavier, now fully in control of himself. He pointed to the ants straddling the high ground. 'All they have to do is wait until the flood water goes down and the river resumes its normal course.'

'*Will* the flood water go down?' asked Jane.

Xavier nodded glumly.

'Surely. It will not take long before the river returns to its natural route again and the dry land soaks up the foot or two of water which the rivulet has spilt. Say, another hour or two at the most.'

'Well,' said Hugo, making some attempt at brevity, 'you could say this respite is a washout . . .'

No one laughed. He did not expect they would.

'So we have an hour or two left?' asked Jane.

'Then we shall be back in the same position, *não e*?' asked Takky.

'They must have some weaknesses,' cried Hugo desperately. 'All right, they are mutants, they have special qualities, but they cannot be all that removed from the ordinary soldier ants and the soldier ants must have some biological weaknesses like all speicies . . . surely?'

It was Chuck who surprised them.

'Excuse me, Senhor Hugo, but these ants . . . I do not think they are exactly *formiga-de-correição*.'

Hugo looked at the boy blankly.

'What do you mean, Chuck?'

'As I say, Senhor Hugo . . . they are not all soldier ants. Look.'

He took a spoon from a rack and managed to scoop up several ants from the water.

Xavier peered closely at them.

'*Deus!*' he breathed suddenly, 'the boy is right, Hugo. We have two different species here. Look, those larger ants are the soldier ants or the *eciton* species. But look at the others . . . the smaller ones. They are a closely related species of *formica-fusca*. Do you know, I believe the soldier ants may not be the *eciton* species after all.'

Hugo sighed deeply.

'I didn't graduate in biology, senhor. What's it mean?'

'Let me try to explain simply . . . I believe these ants are not true soldier ants but the *polygerus* or Amazon Ant. It could even be that the mutation consists of a cross between the *polygerus* and the *eciton* . . .'

'Whoa, you're leaving me behind again.'

Xavier was clearly an enthusiast.

'The *polygerus* or Amazon Ant, my dear Hugo, is commonly called the slave-making ant. The *polygerus* has jaws that are so long and sharp and curved that they are superb for fighting. That is why in aggression and physical appearance the *polygerus* can sometimes be mistaken for soldier ants. But, whereas the soldier ant is self sufficient, the *polygerus* is not. See the long fighting fangs? Those fighting jaws are useless in feeding their offspring and even themselves.'

'Then how do they survive?' demanded Jane.

'Exactly as their name tells you. The *polygerus* capture other ants and trains them as slaves, usually capturing a closely related species like the *formica-fusca*, and each *polygerus* has about six or seven slave ants to sustain it. The slaves are taken in raids which sometimes turn into great battles in which thousands of ants are slain.'

Hugo shook his head in disbelief.

'It sounds like something out of H. G. Wells to me. Pure science fiction.'

Xavier gave an emphatic jerk of his head.

'I can assure you that the *polygerus* is a scientific fact. They occur fairly commonly among Amazon ants.'

'But if what you say is true, and I'm sure it is, we don't know for sure that these mutants are a basic *polygerus* species. And if so, what use is the information to us?'

'I can show you that what the senhor says is true,' interrupted Chuck. He asked Hugo and Xavier to help him replace the ladder to the roof and, taking the field glasses, which Lopez had discarded in the kitchen, he scuttled onto the roof. Hugo and Xavier followed.

'Look through these, Senhor Hugo, over there!'

The boy pointed with a quivering forefinger in the direction of the massing ants.

Through the focused lenses Hugo could now distinctly see, in the early dawn light, what he had failed to see previously. Along the serried columns of large ants were what seemed like channels along which smaller ants moved back and forth, each carrying or pushing twigs towards the front column of ants. Hugo let out a long, low whistle of surprise.

'I guess this is all a crazy dream,' he said turning to Xavier who almost snatched the glasses from him to confirm his premise.

'So,' he said after a few minutes pause, 'they are *polygerus* ants, the slave-making ants. The smaller ants are unfortunates who have been conquered in battle and now obey the commands of the *polygerus*. But there is nothing fantastic in that; such ant societies have stretched back to creation itself.'

Hugo sat in silent thought.

'Senhor,' he suddenly said, 'when the *polygerus* attack other ant colonies to take slaves, is it inevitable that the lesser ants fight back?'

Xavier frowned.

'Do you mean – do ants willingly become slaves of the *polygerus*? The answer is no, of course. No animal willingly becomes the slave of another. The lesser ants always put up a resistance, even if it is sometimes a token one. Sometimes it has been known that the *polygerus* are repulsed but not often.'

Hugo nodded thoughtfully.

'Do I recall you saying that about ten kilometres from here, in the direction of the river, there lay some great ant colonies?'

'That's right,' affirmed Xavier. 'In the arid country to the west, just before you reach the river. But I shouldn't

166

think they are anything to do with these ants . . . I thought so at first but they are *formica-fusca* . . .'

His voice trailed off.

'You have some sort of plan in mind, Hugo,' he asked quietly.

Hugo looked up with an eagerness in his eye.

'It is a very far fetched plan, senhor. But then the whole business is far fetched and unbelievable. There is nothing else I can think of. We must leave here, agreed? We must try to get to the river as we tried to do yesterday.

'Agreed.'

Hugo waved a hand towards the water sodden country-side. Already vast patches of land were beginning to show through the waterlogged areas and the black columns were reforming and pressing nearer.

'My plan is this: we wrap up in whatever protective clothing we can. We take one of the jeeps and try to break through the ants towards the west, towards the river as we tried to do yesterday. The end result will be to try to reach your cabin cruiser and escape to Morená by means of the river. If you look in that direction,' he pointed westward, 'you will see that most of the area is low lying and the ant columns that were there have been washed away. They don't appear to be concentrating on reforming west of the river. Their main concentrations lie to the south and east.'

Xavier shrugged.

'So? Perhaps you are right. Perhaps we can break through there but then what? They will soon cut us off, I think.'

'This is where my idea comes in.'

'Go ahead.'

'One thing I have learnt from history concerning the rise of empires . . . that is an empire is usually founded on the Roman concept *divide et impera*, divide and rule. The concept has always been a foundation stone for man's imperial adventures. But now the same principal could be used for our own salvation.'

'How do you mean?'

Xavier was intrigued.

'If the slave ants can be turned against their masters, we might be able to prevent pursuit and reach the river in safety.'

Xavier smiled wanly.

'You were right before, friend Hugo. Your plan is far fetched. How, precisely, do you plan to accomplish the miracle of turning the slave ants against their masters?'

'If we break out of here, the ant columns will start in pursuit?'

'I am sure of it,' said Xavier.

'Well, we must try to get to the ant colonies to the west. I am working on the assumption that they have not been attacked by the *polygerus* yet. We make for the colonies, drive through them towards the river. I know it's a long shot but, hopefully, the *polygerus* will encounter the colonies and the *formica-fusca*, as you call them, will think they are raiding for slaves. They will fight back tooth and nail . . . or whatever the ant equivalent is. They will defend their territory while we get away in the confusion.'

Xavier laughed sardonically.

'You said it was a far fetched plan. I think it is impossible.'

'What choice is there, Senhor Xavier?'

Jane emerged from the kitchen onto the roof.

'If we stay here, we will be killed. At least Hugo's plan offers a slight hope. As the Americans say – there isn't any other ball game.'

Hugo smiled and clasped her hand.

'Then,' said Xavier, 'the sooner we get started the better. Let's get everything together and let's hope the jeeps haven't become waterlogged.'


## CHAPTER TWENTY-TWO

Twenty minutes later a jeep accelerated away from the house, ploughing through the muddy shallows of what had once been Xavier's spacious lawn. The tyres churned up wads of mud and sent it flying in large clouds behind the vehicle.

Behind the driving wheel Hugo breathed a small prayer of thanks that the waterproofing around the engine had held and that the vehicle seemed completely manoeuvrable. Beside him sat Xavier. On his knees was a large picnic hamper in which lay a number of bottles filled with petrol which had been syphoned from the second jeep. Hugo had spent some time filling these bottles, inserting cotton waste strips and making passable Molotov Cocktails. It was a precaution which he hoped they would not need.

In the back of the jeep Chuck sat between Jane and Takky. They were all covered in an assortment of clothing to protect their bodies and the canvas coverings on the jeep had been fully extended and reinforced.

The jeep skidded to a halt before the remains of the wrecked bridge which used to span the six or so metres of the rivulet, west of the house. The rivulet was still flowing shallowly, following the diaspora of its waters across the valley. Hugo examined the bed of the stream carefully.

'Let's pray that it's not boggy down there,' he muttered. 'Hold on, folks, there's no other way.'

He clashed the jeep into gear and skidded it down the embankment into the stream which, at its deepest point, was not above two feet. The jeep went into the water at a good speed sending spray cascading on all sides. Foot down on the accelerator, Hugo sent the jeep ploughing over the river bed and, with a quick change of the gears, started to push it up the furthest bank.

There was a protesting whine as the back wheel suddenly spun without gripping the muddy bottom.

With a grimace, Hugo took his foot off the accelerator and let the vehicle slide back a little. Then he pressed on the pedal again. The car moved forward a few feet before the telltale whine of a racing engine told him that the back wheel was slipping again.

Takky crossed herself and muttered a prayer.

Hugo let the jeep slide back again and then repeated the operation. The result was entirely the same.

'Hold on!' snapped Xavier, putting down the basket of petrol bombs. He raised the canvas cover and sprang out of the jeep, standing knee deep in the water. He examined the back wheels and then quickly started to collect stones and pieces of wood.

Jane, peering out of the small plastic window at the rear of the jeep, let out an exclamation.

'Hurry, hurry . . . the ants are on the move!'

'Almost finished,' gasped Xavier.

The seconds seemed like an eternity before Xavier was waving Hugo forward. The American depressed the accelerator pedal, slowly the jeep moved forward and began to climb up out of the bed of the rivulet. Once, he felt the wheels slipping again. In his agitation he shot his foot down on the gas which made matters worse. The panic worked his face until he calmed himself and eased up, finding as he did so that the wheels caught against the wood and the stones again.

Then they were onto the bank and Xavier was scrambling in beside him and resuming his precious burden again.

'Let's get to hell out of here,' the plantation owner almost snarled.

Hugo sent the jeep forward in a surge of mud and spray.

There were plenty of ants about: piles of drowned ants lying inert over the watery fields, everywhere there was movement but the groups of ants moving hither and thither from one dry patch of ground to another seemed without leadership or direction, trying to reorganise themselves into the columns which had been devastated by the breaking dam. To Hugo it looked like the aftermath of some great battle with shell-shocked soldiers aimlessly groping this way and that, searching for comrades or their lost regiments with which to regroup. Certainly these ants were of no threat to the jeep or its occupants. The danger seemed to lie behind them.

Xavier was wiping the sweat from his forehead.

'So far so good, eh?' he muttered.

'How far is it to the ant colonies?' asked Hugo.

'About six or seven miles. Keep on the route we took yesterday. They lie along the same road on the arid ground just before the river.'

Hugo was keeping the speed of the jeep down purposely as the floods caused vast patches of mud and now and then the vehicle was sent into a skid from which, had he been travelling faster, it might have overturned.

'It was just up ahead that we saw the ants before,' shouted Jane from the back.

Hugo gave a slight nod as he swung the vehicle around the shoulder of the hill.

The road was clear.

'Senhor! Senhor!'

Takky's voice was cracked and breathless.

'Senhor . . . to the right! Madonna! Look to the right!'

A quick glance caused Hugo to go cold. A long and broad black column, a little ahead and to the right of the roadway, seemed to be pulsating across the ground at an incredible speed, as if to cut off the route of the jeep.

Now sure of firm and drier ground, Hugo pressed the accelerator to the floor boards.

'Hang on tight!' he snapped over his shoulder.

The jeep seemed to leap forward, bumping sickeningly over the trackway. Xavier clutched his incendiary cargo, praying that a sudden bump would not smash and ignite the whole mess.

'Careful, Hugo,' he breathed softly.

One eye on the advancing black column, the other on the speeding trackway, Hugo suddenly realised that the advance guard of the ants would reach the trackway at precisely the same time he would pass by their front. His pilot training had taught him to judge such distances.

'Senhor,' he said to Xavier, 'we are going to pass through the front of the ants. Light two petrol bombs and when I say "now" throw them out. Understand?'

'Yes.'

'Pass the box back to me,' shouted Jane, reaching forward.

Xavier passed back the picnic hamper and, with his hands thus freed, he was able to take two of the bottles and, with his cigarette lighter, ignite the fuse. He swung back the canvas cover of the jeep and held the bottles ready.

'Now!' screamed Hugo.

The two petrol bombs exploded with a roar of flame. Momentarily the ants stopped their forward advance as hundreds of them were incinerated by the spreading fiery liquid.

The jeep sped past the column. Even so, several ants had managed to attach themselves to the vehicle and Xavier was trying to beat them off the canvas covering.

The vehicle sped on towards a meandering stream which seemed to rise in the tall hills to the north and make a slow progression towards the southern valleys. The road spanned the stream by means of a tiny wooden bridge.

Once across the bridge, Hugo halted the jeep.

'Two petrol bombs on the bridge, burn it,' he ordered brusquely. 'It will hold up the ants for a while. They'll have to swim across the stream.'

Within seconds the old wooden bridge was a burning inferno and the jeep was speeding on.

Behind them Jane could see the hills acrawl with black columns.

She felt too sick to even shudder.

'How much further?' she whispered.

'There are the ant colonies!' cried Xavier, pointing to large sand hill affairs which spread for some distance across the valley bottom, a dry, arid stretch of country, not dissimilar to a desert. Beyond this stretch of sand and mud, Hugo could see the verdant foliage which marked the passage of the river.

'Let's hope your idea works,' muttered Xavier. 'Let's hope these ants are disposed to fight our *polygerus* friends!'

Hugo gave a tight-lipped grin.

'It's a bit late in the day to start worrying about that now.'

There were no signs of the colonist ants as the jeep ploughed through the vast sand fields in which the colonies had been erected. They were great dune-like affairs which rose to a height of twenty feet and, spread over the area, there must have been at least a hundred such dunes.

Hugo wove the jeep carefully through the structures.

Jane looked behind them and bit her lip.

'They're coming!'

The hills behind them were now the colour of pitch. It was as if someone had taken a bottle of black ink and simply thrown it across the once green and brown countryside.

'Look! Look!' cried Chuck. 'The ants!'

The little boy was not pointing to the menacing black mass behind them but at the sand dunes.

'*Deus!*' cried Xavier, 'but I think your idea might be working, my friend!'

From the dunes thousands of little red ants were pouring in a steady stream and moving off in masses towards the threatening black mass. The whole area of dunes was erupting in a sea of red.

Before the jeep plunged into the gloomy coverage of the rain forest, Jane caught a brief glimpse of a small patch of red hurling itself into the slow moving and irresistible black sea.

Then they were among the trees and tearing down a forest trackway.

'Poor creatures,' said Xavier softly, 'they haven't a hope against the *polygerus* but they will fight while they can.'

'And gain time for us to escape,' observed Hugo.

'Indeed. Your divide and survive theory works, *não e*?'

'Better wait to say that until we are safe at Morená,' replied Hugo. 'Which way is it to your boathouse?'

'Just round this bend . . . ah, here is the river.'

They scrambled out of the jeep before a wooden structure which jutted out into the river. In the excitement of the escape, Xavier had forgotten to bring his keys and he and Hugo were forced to smash in the door. Inside, resting lightly in the water, was Xavier's thirty-five foot cabin cruiser.

'Get aboard, everyone,' cried Xavier. 'Hugo, can you

take the controls while I warm up the engines? There's enough petrol aboard, I think, to get us safely to Morená.'

Hugo nodded and shepherded Jane, Takky and Chuck below. He then cast off the ropes and pushed the boat out of the boathouse and let it gently nose down the river. Then he climbed to the tiny cockpit and examined the controls. They were fairly simple.

Below, he could hear the cough of the engines. Suddenly, after a few false starts, the engines gave a full-throated roar and then settled down to a gentle purr.

Xavier, grease on his face, emerged on the tiny bridge.

'We'll have to wait for a few minutes before we can open up the throttle. The engines will take a while to warm up.'

Hugo pointed grimly to the shore line.

'I don't think we have a few minutes, senhor,' he said quietly.

The bank was black with ants.

Xavier's face paled.

'Secure the doors below!' he roared at Jane, who was peering curiously out of the cabin door.

She hesitated, saw a cloud of anger gathering on Hugo's face, turned and shut the door.

Xavier bent over the controls and eased the throttle open.

The engine misfired a couple of times, coughed, missed and then picked up in a half-hearted fashion.

Gradually the screws of the boat began to push the craft into mid-river.

Ants were now falling on the decks of the boat in their hundreds, seeming to leap from over hanging branches, or outgrowing undergrowth and bushes.

Hugo stamped at them viciously. They seemed to get everywhere, crawling in their tiny groups towards Xavier and him.

He felt parts of his flesh on fire, his legs, chest and arms, and looking down he saw hundreds of black ants crawling across his body. It was the same with Xavier who was trying to manoeuvre the craft away from the ant-clotted banks with one hand while slapping at the creatures with his other hand.

Hugo spied a fire extinguisher on the side of the boat, grabbed it and levelled it at Xavier. Within seconds the ants were washed from his body. Ignoring his own pain, Hugo ran over the boat, flushing away the ants that had succeeded in landing on it. Finally, he turned the spluttering extinguisher on himself and breathed a prayer of relief for the cold water which anaesthetised his agonised flesh.

Gasping his relief, Hugo looked round.

Xavier had succeeded in getting the boat out in mid-river beyond the reaches of the silent black masses on the western bank.

Even then, tiny groups of ants were trying to get to the boat, pushing out from the bank on leaves, twigs and other floatable objects. But the craft was going too fast now.

As Hugo looked on the serried black ranks he had a strange feeling; he seemed to hear the high pitched tinkle of crystal, the faint rising and falling of surf on a sea shore. The noise rose and then fell. It was rather like a human sigh.


Two days later they were in Moraná and had told their tale to an incredulous government official. Only Xavier's standing in the community – so Hugo felt – prevented the official from having them thrown out of his office as people who were obviously *louco* or *demente*! Three hours later, a helicopter having made a reconnaissance over the area, a horrified pilot reported the incredible spectacle of a mass of ants covering many square kilometres moving in the vicinity of Xavier's plantation.

The official nervously bowed them out of his office.

'It is a job for the Air Force to destroy them,' he muttered. 'Leave everything in our hands.'

Outside the government building it was a hot June day. The little town of Moraná nestled peacefully by the Xingu River, its people going about their respective businesses unaware of the terrifying manifestation two days journey to the south of them.

Senhor de Silva Xavier looked on with a sadly shaking head.

'Incredible,' he whispered.

'What will you do?' enquired Hugo, standing by his side with Jane. Takky and Chuck had gone back to the rooming house where Xavier had hired accommodation for them.

'I?' smiled the plantation owner at the young couple. 'I will go back when the Air Force has cleared the countryside.'

'But surely you would not return to the plantation?' asked an incredulous Jane.

'Where else should I go, Senhorinha Jane?' asked the man, with dignity. 'The family of de Silva Xavier have held that land for generations. They have encountered many problems in the past and will doubtless encounter many more in the future. Acts of God, nature, man-made disasters, the family have survived them all. It will take more than a swarm of mutant ants to wrest my home, my land, my livelihood from me.'

Hugo nodded sympathetically.

'But after . . . after . . .' Jane faltered.

'The de Silva Xaviers are people of the land, my dear senhorinha,' said the old man gently. 'People of the land must always fight disaster, they must fight droughts, they must fight floods, they must fight fires. They worry when a day is too hot, they worry when a day is too cold, they worry when there is nothing to worry about. That is the life of a man who works the land. I would have it no other way.'

He sighed.

'Poor Conseulo. She could never understand that fact.'

He looked at Jane and Hugo in turn.

'I *did* love her, you know. But my love was not enough for her. She was my wife but my land was my mistress. It will always be so.'

He pulled at his lower lip and was lost in thought for a moment, the hint of a tear glistening in his eye.

'And what will you do, friend Hugo,' he suddenly said, pulling himself up. 'Can I not persuade you to stay with me? I will even buy you that new aeroplane that you so badly wanted.'

Hugo grinned and let his arm slip round Jane's waist.

'It is a tempting offer, sir. And I am really grateful but I have a better plan in mind. I'm going home to Seattle to join a civilian airline company . . . I'm going to settle down . . . and I'm going to get married if the lady will have me.'

Jane looked up at him quickly and smiled.

'The lady will,' she said softly.

Xavier leant forward and took their hands in his.

'I understand. Luck go with you. I am happy for you.'

He paused as a shadow of a frown crossed his forehead.

'Have you told the boy, Uuatsim, young Chuck, as you call him? He is very attached to you.'

'I have told him I shall be returning to my country,' said Jane. 'Stupidly, I even suggested that he could come with me but he proved himself to be more mature than I am. He said that he knew of the white man's great villages of stone and how could I expect him to leave his forests for such places? He even asked me how I could return to a white village, he meant city, after I had seen the way in which men should truly live, free in the bosom of their mother, the earth? He asked how anyone could breath the foul air or sleep with the terrible noises of the traffic? He asked how could they eat the food which was made to have tastes which were not its own – a fair comment on what we call sophisticated western cooking.'

She hesitated.

'Do you know, I didn't know how to answer him?'

Xavier let out his breath in a long sigh.

'The boy seems to have wisdom beyond his years. But if he will stay here, then there is always a home for him with me and Takky who will return with me when I go back.'

'I think young Chuck will like that,' agreed Jane.

'Good. When do you leave?'

'Tomorrow morning,' replied Hugo promptly. 'There's a flight to Cuiaba and then we will go on to Rio.'

'Very well. As much as I regret your going, we shall make dinner this evening a meal worth remembering, *não e?*'

He turned abruptly, his eyes glistening and walked away.

Arm in arm, Hugo and Jane walked through the market town, absorbed in each other's company with that selfishness that only the first flush of love displays.


## CHAPTER TWENTY-THREE

Across an azure sky, nine tiny black specks sped so swiftly that the eye of a human observer could scarcely distinguish their passage. At 39,000 feet above the jungles of the Matto Grosso, Major Pinhiero Manachado of the Brazilian Air Force felt the throbbing of his Atar 9c engine. He glanced casually at the controls of his Mirage IIIe single seater interceptor.

There was a brief crackle of static in his earphones.

'Red leader . . . red leader . . . this is São Paulo control. Come in, red leader.'

Manachado flicked a switch.

'Red leader to São Paulo base, acknowledging.'

'Confirm your ETA, red leader. Over.'

Manachado looked at his air speed indicator and checked off some figures on the writing pad strapped to his right leg.

'Red leader to São Paulo base. Estimated Time of Arrival on target area will be twelve forty-one hours. Now at zero minus five minutes.'

'Acknowledged, red leader. Out.'

Bloody fools, thought Manachado, as he glanced around making sure the accompanying eight Mirage IIIe's of his squadron were in position. As if São Paulo coordinators could not work out an ETA for the squadron by themselves. The pilot watched the minutes tick off on his clock, thinking of nothing in particular and certainly not the job in hand. He was too well trained to give his mission any apprehensive thought.

'Red leader calling all sections. Reduce speed. Target coming up.'

A chorus of acknowledgement punctuated the static of his earphones.

Manachado, followed closely by his squadron, eased his interceptor down to fifteen thousand feet.

'Red leader to all sections. Target area ahead. I repeat, target area ahead. There's our back-up squadron.'

Circling over the area just above them Manachado's trained eye had picked up twelve Cessna AT 37c light attack aircraft.

Again the static crackled.

'São Paulo base to red leader. Have you a fix on blue leader? Do you see him? Over?'

'Affirmative, São Paulo.'

'Okay, red leader. Blue leader is above target area and has laid out flares. Switch to inter-aircraft communication. Your control is now visual.'

'Check, São Paulo.'

Manachado switched to the new radio wave band, waited until the short burst of static had died away and then gave his call sign.

'Roger, red leader,' came a voice. 'Blue leader reading you loud and clear.'

'Where's the target, friend?' demanded Manachado.

There was a barking like noise. Manachado thought it was the static until he realised that the Cessna pilot was laughing.

'Take your pick, red leader. You've got about five square kilometres of target area below. Anywhere on the black area . . . the black is the ants.'

'Acknowledged, blue leader,' replied Manachado coldly. 'Stand by.'

He flicked his radio transmission switch again.

'Red leader to all sections . . . circle at ten thousand. I'm going down for a recce.'

As the chorus died away, Manachado pushed his stick

forward so that the Mirage side slipped towards the ground. As he dropped closer, the pilot let the breath whistle through his teeth in disbelief. The Cessna pilot had not been kidding. Across the hills to the extent of five or more kilometres there was nothing but a sea of blackness. The only terrain he could identify were the larger mounds or hills. Everything else was covered in black against which the only relief was the occasional flash of a red pin point here and there as the sun caught at the millions of reddy black insects which must make up the colossal spectacle.

Manachado pulled back the stick and climbed rapidly back to his circling formation in bewilderment. At the briefing he had been told, by an ironic intelligence officer, that the squadron were going to help out some farmers by laying napalm on some swarms of ants which had gotten out of hand. He was told to expect a fairly considerable swarm of soldier ants or some similar species but he had never expected anything quite so large, so terrifying, as the area which the creatures now covered.

'Red leader to all sections. The first section will follow me and we will commence napalming the northern flank. That should blow the flames right across the area. Okay?'

'Roger, red leader,' came the acknowledgements.

'Let's go! Let's go!' shouted Manachado.

The Mirage interceptors swung down and began a bombing run along the northern edge of the black mass.

Half an hour later the entire area was ablaze, the smoke could be seen as far away as Morená.

At dawn the next morning three helicopters took off from Morená and flew a reconnaissance sortie over the area looking for signs of movement.

The pilots reported back in high spirits that they could see nothing but blackened brush, burnt out trees and scorched earth. There was no sign of life anywhere.

'Look's like Manachado's boys have wiped the blasted things off the face of the earth,' chortled the major in command. 'They seemed to have frizzled right up. No sign of anything moving anywhere. We're coming home now.'

At 21,000 feet, the DC10 of Pan American Airlines stopped climbing and the cool, efficient air hostesses bustled about serving drinks.

Hugo smiled, perhaps a little sadly, at Jane.

'Goodbye, Brazil,' he whispered.

Jane turned and looked through the window at the white clouds, floating like so much cotton wool a few feet below them.

'I know what you mean,' she said finally. 'I seem to have spent an eternity here. Poor father. I could never bring myself to continue his researches now.'

Hugo squeezed her hand.

'Now then. Think positive thoughts, eh? A new life and a new career. We'll be in Seattle soon . . . a new home.'

Jane smiled back.

'All the same, I can't help thinking what is going to happen to little Chuck and Xavier and Takky . . . I would never have returned to that plantation after, after . . .'

She shuddered slightly.

Hugo was reassuring.

'After the Brazilian Air Force have knocked the hell out of those mutants, it will be as safe as houses. Mind you, I don't want anyone to mention the word "ant" to me for a very long time. I hope some guy up at the Pentagon will start thinking again before they let those B52s roam around the globe loaded with bombs. It's the second B52 crash I know of . . . I remember a few years back a SAC bomber, carrying a primed nuclear payload, crashed off the Spanish coast. Jesus! Just imagine if the radiation leaked into the Atlantic and started causing mutations among the sea life . . .!'

'Anyway,' Jane was emphatic, 'it's over now and, as you say, I don't want to hear the word "ant" for a long time to come.'

Hugo nodded and ordered two brandies from a hovering air hostess.

A few miles to the south of the great area of devastation, a general was watching the remnants of his soldiers making a bivouac for the night. The directions which had gone out to the soldiers, as they prepared the bivouac, was to prepare it for a stay of several days for the queen, whom they accompanied, was heavy in pregnancy and would start laying her eggs within the next few hours. Soon, the general hoped, his swarm would be reinforced with new troops for the progression from egg to lava, lava to pupa and pupa to adult would not take long.

As he watched the reddy black columns of soldiers march by carrying twigs and leaves to reinforce their bivouac, the general raised up his large head and waved his two elbowed antennae in satisfaction.

Soon his soldier ants would be strong enough to march once more against the puny man-things who felt themselves masters of the earth and lords of the future. In the few square kilometres of the surrounding forest there were more ants than there were men in the world. Each ant lived in a close ordered society. Each ant was possessed of intelligence, of discipline. Now the ants were evolving, storing knowledge as men did, and forming ambitions . . . the ambition to be masters of the environment.

The general rubbed his antennae together.

Soon. Soon . . .

# THE VENGEANCE OF SHE

They called her 'She-Who-Must-Be-Obeyed' – priestess of the ancient Mother of Mysteries, whose story had become a terrifying legend. Her body had perished thousands of years ago, but her spirit was immortal, and she had sworn one day to return and wreak havoc on those who had destroyed her.

Dr Hugh Strickland didn't believe in dusty old legends. But when pretty young Noreen Pemberton was entrusted to his psychiatric care, he was forced to rethink all his long-held beliefs. For another personality was fighting for possession of Noreen's body.

As the invading spirit grew stronger, Strickland realized that he was dealing with something monstrous and beyond his control – and that knowledge put him in mortal danger. For, fuelled by the fires of a long forgotten age, Ayesha was rising – to fulfil her legend and live again!

0 7221 8579 0      FICTION/HORROR

85p

And selected from the
SPHERE Horror List

## THE DEVIL'S MAZE

GERALD SUSTER

The Black Lodge has met. In the treacherous, flitting
shadow-world that exists on the fringes of 'respectable'
Victorian London, a 'Blood Quest' is being arranged.
The malevolent Dr Lipsius and his voracious disciples
have picked their victims. Now the death-trap must be
baited with sweet and tempting lures, in order that the
Darkness may do battle with the Light.

Soon, a man and a woman will enter a deadly labyrinth.
Perverse pleasure, dark designs and sinister forces: all
will lead back to the black heart of THE DEVIL'S
MAZE . . .

Superlatively chilling . . . brilliant in its summoning-up of
an Age of Evil . . . here is a shattering novel of dark
forces that will take its place as a new classic of occult
horror.

0 7221 8286 4     FICTION/HORROR

85p

# ELIZABETH

JESSICA HAMILTON

'If you were to go into your bedroom tonight – perhaps by candlelight – and sit quietly before the large mirror, you might see what I have seen. Sit patiently, looking neither at yourself nor at the glass. You might notice that the image is not yours, but that of an exceptional person who lived at some other time . . .'

The image in the mirror of fourteen-year-old Elizabeth Cuttner is that of the fey and long-dead Frances, who introduces Elizabeth to her chilling world of the supernatural. Through Frances, Elizabeth learns what it is to wield power – power of a kind that is malevolent and seemingly invincible. Power that begins with the killing of her parents . . .

'An elegant study of a world in which evil is total and totally triumphant.' – *The Sunday Times*

0 7221 4285 4     FICTION/HORROR

75p

# A selection of Bestsellers from Sphere Books

*Fiction*

| | | | |
|---|---|---|---|
| THE WOMEN'S ROOM | Marilyn French | £1.50p | ☐ |
| SINGLE | Harriet Frank | £1.10p | ☐ |
| THE BENEDICT ARNOLD CONNECTION | | | |
| | Joseph DiMona | 95p | ☐ |
| CHARNEL HOUSE | Graham Masterton | 85p | ☐ |
| THIS RAVAGED HEART | Barbara Riefe | £1.25p | ☐ |
| EXIT SHERLOCK HOLMES | Robert Lee Hall | 95p | ☐ |
| DEATH OF AN EXPERT WITNESS | P. D. James | 95p | ☐ |

*Film and Television Tie-ins*

| | | | |
|---|---|---|---|
| THE PASSAGE | Bruce Nicolaysen | 95p | ☐ |
| INVASION OF THE BODY SNATCHERS | | | |
| | Jack Finney | 85p | ☐ |
| THE EXPERIMENT | John Urling Clark | 95p | ☐ |

*Non-Fiction*

| | | | |
|---|---|---|---|
| HOME FARM | Michael Allaby & Colin Tudge | £2.50p | ☐ |
| THE JENNIFER PROJECT | Clyde W. Burleson | 95p | ☐ |
| THE SEXUAL CONNECTION | John Sparks | 85p | ☐ |
| ELEPHANTS IN THE LIVING ROOM, | | | |
| BEARS IN THE CANOE | Earl & Liz Hammond | £1.25p | ☐ |
| IN HIS IMAGE | David Rorvik | £1.00p | ☐ |
| THE MUSICIANS OF AUSCHWITZ | | | |
| | Fania Fenelon | 95p | ☐ |

*All Sphere books are available at your local bookshop or newsagent, or can be ordered direct from the publisher. Just tick the titles you want and fill in the form below.*

Name.............................................................................................................................

Address .......................................................................................................................

...................................................................................................................................

Write to Sphere Books, Cash Sales Department, P.O. Box 11, Falmouth, Cornwall TR10 9EN

Please enclose cheque or postal order to the value of the cover price plus:

UK: 22p for the first book plus 10p per copy for each additional book ordered to a maximum charge of 82p

OVERSEAS: 30p for the first book and 10p for each additional book

BFPO & EIRE: 22p for the first book plus 10p per copy for the next 6 books, thereafter 4p per book

*Sphere Books reserve the right to show new retail prices on covers which may differ from those previously advertised in the text or elsewhere, and to increase postal rates in accordance with the GPO.*

(4:79)